THE SAPPHIRE CIRCLET

A Sherwood & Jarvis Novella

Case No. 2

RENEE EDWARDS

To my mother Pam,
who appreciates a nice bit of bling

FROM THE DIARY OF WILFRED A. JARVIS, M.D.,
ARMY MEDICAL DEPARTMENT,
OFFICE OF THE MILITARY ATTACHÉ TO THE
AMBASSADOR,
YNIS WITRIN

Chapter 1

21 May 1881

DEAR ESTHER—

There have been very few days that one might call "normal" since I arrived here in Ynis Witrin, but I should have known this one would be particularly irregular when it began with me being lectured by an indignant brownie.

I was going about my morning routine, taking special care for reasons that will become clear, when there was a knock at my front door. Perplexed and not a little annoyed, I answered it, only to find the space before me empty. I was on the brink of slamming the door and dispensing with the final tasks that would get me out of the house when I heard a cough. Looking down, I saw the brownie—one of those small Folk who carry out much of the labor on the island—outfitted in a neat black dress and cap, with a pair of spectacles on her nose and a rather garish carpetbag in her hand. She peered at me over the rims of her glasses.

"Are you Dr. Jarvis, then?"

"Er, yes," I said, somewhat taken aback by her abrupt manner.

"My name is Carys Rhiannon Howell," she said. "You may refer to me as Mrs. Howell. I am to be your housekeeper."

"I'm sorry," I said, baffled. "But I have not engaged a housekeeper."

"Be that as it may," she said. "I *was* engaged, and now I am here, and I am ready to work. If you would be so good as to let me in, I will get started."

"Now see here, Mrs…" I began, then realized I had lost track of her name in attempting to figure out what the blazes was going on.

"Howell," she supplied, with more than a touch of condescension.

"Mrs. Howell. I think there has been some sort of mistake. I put out no request for a housekeeper. I have not even thought of doing so. Your services are not required here."

In response, the tiny woman planted her feet on the stone, crossed her arms, and glared at me.

"Dr. Jarvis," she said. "I am an honest woman. I work hard to earn my bread, and I hold to my commitments. No one can say that I don't."

"Of course," I said, feeling unaccountably chastened. "I didn't mean to imply—"

"I was hired to manage this house. Whoever did the hiring is no concern of mine. I only know that I agreed to do the work, and the work, I intend to do."

I opened my mouth for one last contestation, but just then, the clock struck the hour, proclaiming that I was late for work. I did not have time to stand there arguing, so I conceded, stepping back and gesturing for Mrs. Howell to enter.

"Deepest apologies, Mrs. Howell," I said. "Do please come in."

She gave a triumphant sniff and swept past me, muttering what I'm sure were very unflattering things under her breath. Soon enough, though, she left off that endeavor in favor of another that was hardly more complimentary. Depositing her bag on the floor next to the coat rack, she turned to take in the state of the parlor, and her face froze in a rictus of horror.

"Oh, but it is worse than I thought," she said, pressing a hand to her mouth, and I decided I had had enough.

"I am due at the office," I said. "We can get this situation sorted out when I return. In the meantime, I do not consider you under any obligation to work. Please make yourself at home."

The last was, I confess, uttered through clenched teeth, but it turned out to be futile regardless. Even as I retreated to the bedroom to complete my toilet, I saw her rolling up her sleeves with a determined gleam in her eye. I decided to deal with it later. My dance card was already full, so to speak.

As I crossed the lawn to the attaché's office, I pondered who could have been responsible for sending this rather domineering woman my way. Could it have been a member of the office staff? Col. Abercrombie seemed unlikely; why would he concern himself with such a trivial matter? Pryce seemed a more promising candidate, but he is a conscientious sort; he definitely would have alerted me beforehand. The odds of Waddington taking on a chore of that type were so vanishingly small they didn't even bear considering. So, who could it have been?

As I reached the office door, I set the question aside for consideration at a later time. I knew I was going to need to keep my wits about me as we continued making preparations for Queen Victoria's birthday.

I know you, like me, must have fond memories of these annual celebrations, but I have come to realize those remembrances are so pleasant because we were not in charge of organizing the festivities. For me, that is no longer the case. The queen's birthday is a great event here on the island, with even more parties, fetes, and amusements planned than normal, something I had previously not believed was possible. The merrymaking is set to last for the full week leading up to Her Majesty's actual birthday on the 24th, at which point there will be a ball and grand illumination to close things out. It is apparently traditional for a representative of the royal family to attend, and Princess Beatrice will make the appearance this year. The British Quarter is abuzz with excitement, but this whole spectacle has created a staggering amount of administrative work, including for us at the attaché's office, despite the fact that it is in no way related to our duties. That meant I had a lot to do once I reached the office, especially since I had been given permission to leave early that day to call upon my friend Miss Sherwood and her family.

Upon the conclusion of our investigation into Enoch Drebber's murder, Miss Sherwood had intimated that we might see each other again soon, even without the demands of the investigation to bring us together, and she had been correct. I came to dread social events less, knowing there was a possibility that she would be present, and we have been able to spend some rather pleasant evenings together, albeit with dozens of our friends and colleagues. I truly do find her excellent company, so when she proposed that I should call at her residence to meet her family, I was deeply gratified, but also rather intimidated.

Her parents are both such singular, impressive individuals —a fierce warrior on the one hand, an explorer and national hero on the other—I worried that I might not be up to snuff as one of their daughter's associates. She must have noticed some of my worries, for she laid a hand on my arm and said in a tone of gentle chiding, "There is no need to fear—they do not bite."

I shrugged her hand away, feeling my cheeks warm in embarrassment. "I know. But they are just so... illustrious. I feel rather drab in comparison.'

She shook her head. "Now you are being ridiculous. And I worry that you will also be disappointed, for they are actually quite pedestrian and ordinary. If you saw Papa sleep-rumpled and scowling at us all over breakfast, your romantic illusions would vanish instantly, never to return."

I felt the corner of my mouth quirk up, almost against my will.

"But in all seriousness," she said. "I would very much like you to meet them. And Constancia is coming home for the birthday celebrations, so that would be the perfect opportunity."

Despite my reservations, I found that I was unable to refuse, especially with the prospect of encountering the famous Constancia Sherwood. Miss Sherwood adores her sister and speaks of her often. Based on those descriptions, Miss Constancia had consistently struck me as someone worth meeting.

And today was the day. But first: work.

As it was still early, I was unsurprised to find both Col. Abercrombie and Waddington absent. Pryce was, equally unsurprisingly, present and accounted for. To a degree, the preparations for the princess's visit have shown Pryce to his best advantage, what with his penchant for orderliness and impatience with nonsense, but even he seemed to be wearing a bit thin; his eyes had begun to glaze over when forced to review yet another guest list. Lord knows it could have been worse. Our previous efforts had helped to bring the Drebber affair to, if not a happy conclusion, at least a satisfactory one, and ease tensions between the Folk and human populations on the island, which is why we were planning parties and not bracing for the dissolution of diplomatic relations. But navigating the intricacies of court politics could still be exceedingly tedious.

I had been in the office only a short time when I was summoned to make a house call for a baby who was feeling poorly. Once I returned, I had just settled in to work on some typing, when Pryce came out into the reception area, hat under his arm and a scowl on his face.

"Are you still planning to head out early today?" he said.

"Yes," I said. "I am supposed to be at the Sherwood residence no later than three o'clock."

He nodded. "I'll do my best to be back by then, but if I'm not, you should go ahead and take your leave."

"You're going out?"

He nodded again, lip curling slightly. "I've been summoned."

"Summoned?" I said. "Summoned where?"

"The castle. The courtiers in charge of the ball have apparently been butting heads with the secretary ambassador's office over some issue or other related to the princess's visit, and Robin Goodfellow sent me a request to step in as mediator."

"What's the trouble now?" I said, and he sighed.

"He was vague on the particulars—something about a bauble the princess is supposed to wear?" He shook his head, making a sound of disgust. "I did not enter the diplomatic service to plan parties and soothe hurt feelings.

The sooner we see the back of this farce, the better." And with that, he clapped his hat on his head and stormed out the door.

I could hardly blame him. I remember Father often commenting that capability could be its own sort of curse; that once it's been established that you are reliable and competent, everyone turns to you in times of need. This has definitely been the case with Pryce over the last few weeks. I made a mental note to pick up a bottle of his favored brandy the next time I am in Glastonbury—spirits to lift his spirits, ha!—then turned my attention once more to the typewriter.

As I worked, I noticed movement in the doorway leading back to the private offices. I paused, glancing that way to identify what had caught my attention, but the doorway was empty. I went back to typing, and a few moments later, I caught sight of the movement again. Again, I paused but could detect nothing amiss. I started typing once more, and sure enough, I saw the movement, but this time, I was also quick enough to catch a glimpse of Waddington darting into the gloom of the hallway. With a sigh, I pushed back from the desk.

"Waddington," I called. "If there is something you need, you may as well come out with it."

At first, all was still, but then Waddington came slinking through the doorway, like some scolded yet unrepentant dog. He crossed over to the desk and dropped into the chair next to it with a rather dejected air. Getting a better look at his face, I was taken aback by the state of him. You can probably surmise by now that it is not unusual for Waddington to report to work looking somewhat the worse for wear; his drunken exploits have been well documented. But something about him seemed different today. His eyes were a bit more sunken, his face more drawn.

For a moment, he said nothing, forcing me to eventually clear my throat and ask, "Well?"

He fiddled with the loose button on his cuff. "Did I hear Pryce say that you are seeing Miss Sherwood today?"

"You did," I said, arching an eyebrow. Considering their history, it was more than a little peculiar that he would be asking after her. They had not, as you might recall, parted on good terms.

He withdrew an envelope from his coat, placed it on the desk, and slid it towards me.

"Would you be so good as to deliver this to her?"

Now I gazed at him in wordless shock, but he purposefully avoided making eye contact. I picked up the missive and examined it. It had already been sealed and bore no exterior marks indicating its purpose. Had Waddington intended to deliver it himself before catching wind of my imminent visit? What could possibly have driven him to such a thing? In any case, if there was malicious intent to the letter, I could not tell. And there was something about Waddington's demeanor that suggested otherwise. His typical arrogance was nowhere in evidence; he seemed almost regretful. This was costing him something. It was enough to make me suppress my instinctive urge to needle him about it.

"Of course," I said instead and slipped the envelope into my own jacket.

He nodded and rose without another word. Shaking my head, I went back to my typing, doing my best to keep from glancing at the clock at the conclusion of every line. It seemed to take a geologic age, but eventually the hands crept around to half-past two—time for me to leave for my call with Miss Sherwood and her family.

As I made my way through the Folk commercial district and up to the castle, I found myself caught up in a series of imagined scenarios, each representing a different way the upcoming meeting might unfold. I typically consider myself a man of even temper and sober judgment, but in this case, my fancies got away from me; they became more farfetched and hyperbolic as they went, anxious as I was to be prepared for any eventuality. In some, the audience was a rousing success, in others, a wretched failure. Lost as I was in my thoughts, the trip seemed to take only a fraction of its usual time, and I felt an unaccustomed stab of nerves when the palace gate came into view. The guards ushered me through with barely a glance, but rather than proceeding along my normal route to the castle proper, I veered off to the side toward the Sherwood residence.

Owing to her position as captain of the Queen's Guard —or, as they are called in Welsh, the Gwragedd Annwn — General Caelia is allocated a private residence on the castle grounds. As I approached the house, I felt much as I had in school, striving to impress the older boys. Reminding myself that I am, in fact, a grown man, soldier, and medical doctor diminished my anxiety, but did not fully dispel it. Upon reaching the door, I knocked before I could talk myself out of it and stepped back to await admittance.

When the door opened, I was greeted by a brownie woman who exuded poise and capability (unlike the one who was doing heaven only knew what to my own house at that moment). She gestured me into the slate-floored entry and took my hat, telling me that the family would receive me in the sitting room. Just as we were setting out, though, a voice hailed us from further along the hall, and I turned to see a smiling General Caelia striding toward us.

She was not wearing her armor, but she was dressed in

trousers, a practice I to which I have still not become accustomed. I realized as she got closer that she also wore a loose linen shirt and tall, immaculately polished boots, very much like the ones her daughter had worn on the night we met. Even aside from her clothing, the general seemed softer here in her home than she typically did when I saw her in the throne room. Her hair was worked into a complicated series of braids common among the warrior women of the court—and some men—which was a marked departure from Miss Sherwood's typical simplicity, but I could see a greater resemblance between mother and daughter than I had noticed before. The general was a sharper, more angular version of Miss Sherwood, but there was some of the same fierce intelligence to their eyes.

"Welcome, doctor," she said.

"General," I said and bowed.

"Oh, don't bother yourself with those kinds of formalities, please," she said. "We are rather more relaxed here."

"Yes, ma'am," I said, worried that I had already gotten off on the wrong foot—of all the scenes I'd imagined, this had not been one of them. But she seemed cheerful enough as she turned to the housekeeper and said, "You may get back to your duties, Mrs. Perry. I will escort Dr. Jarvis to the sitting room."

"Yes, ma'am." Mrs. Perry inclined her head in farewell and disappeared into the house.

"We have all been looking forward to meeting you," the general said as we walked. "Honoria speaks of you so highly."

I felt myself flush, both proud and humbled. "I think quite highly of her as well, ma'am."

She smiled. "I believe you. And I am glad. She is a solitary girl, our Honoria, particularly when her sister is away, which is the case so often now. I worry sometimes that she spends rather too much time alone, but that seems to have changed since she's met you."

I was at a loss for how to respond to this statement, but luckily, we seemed to have reached our destination. Without ceremony, General Caelia reached for the door-knob and swung open the door to the sitting room.

The room was comfortably furnished and warmly inviting—I would even go so far as to say cozy. The stone walls were hung with tapestries in shades of green and blue, which were interrupted every so often by bookshelves. The floor was layered with intricate carpets, and a hand-some leather sofa and set of matching armchairs were arranged in front of the massive fireplace, along with a tea table. Across the room, there was a large wooden desk and another group of armchairs alongside a wooden globe and a glass case filled with insect specimens and samples of fauna. I assumed these were souvenirs from Sir Arthur's travels; indeed, there were many fascinating objects scat-tered around the room that I recognized from Father's books on South America and Oceania.

In one armchair near the globe, a figure dressed in trousers and shirtsleeves—presumably the intrepid explorer in question—sat partially hidden behind a news-paper that, like most that reached the island, was several days old. If he had noticed our entrance, he gave no indi-cation. The general cleared her throat, but still, the man in the chair did not respond.

"Dearest," she said finally, a touch of reproach in her voice. "Dr. Jarvis is here."

With an exasperated sigh, the reader flipped down a corner of the paper, revealing his face. Sir Arthur Sher-wood is much what one would expect. "Ruggedly hand-some" is, I believe, the term some fawning journalist might use to describe him, and well, they would not be wrong.

His skin is weathered from his time at sea, but in a way that speaks of vitality rather than weariness and overwork. His hair is longer than would be considered fashionable or even respectable in most circles and tinged with grey, as is his beard, and, of course, he wears the famous leather patch over his left eye. The overall effect is quite piratical.

"What are you on about, my love?" he said, with a combination of affection and harried annoyance.

The general was still smiling, but the expression had gone rather tighter than before. "Dr. Jarvis," she said. "Remember, Honoria invited him to call today."

For a moment, he went on gazing at her blankly, but then realization struck him, and his demeanor transformed.

"Of course!" He closed the paper and set it aside, then got to his feet and extended his hand. "Good to meet you, doctor! Our daughter has told us so much about you."

"Thank you, sir," I said as I shook his hand. "It is a pleasure to meet you as well." And it was. You know, Esther, that I am not one who is prone to hero worship, but I found myself strangely giddy in Sir Arthur's presence. After all, he was a figure out of our most beloved child-hood stories, just as iconic as Queen Mab and Robin Goodfellow, if not more so, because he was our country-man. In person, he demonstrates an affecting (if unsurprising) prestige that commands attention. For all the swashbuckling idiosyncrasies, he has the easy authority and confident swagger of one born to wealth and privilege. Though I suppose he would have to be possessed of more than a little bravado to prove a match for his wife.

The general bade us sit, and we spent the next quarter of an hour in most pleasant conversation. Miss Sherwood's parents proved both erudite and witty, which was in no way unexpected, but gratifying nonetheless. I was particularly taken with the stories of Miss Sherwood's childhood that they shared with me.

"Always with her head in a book, that one," Sir Arthur said at length. "Even when I ran the girls out of doors for fresh air and recreation, she would smuggle some tome or other out upon her person. And Constancia would always come to her defense, deflecting my attention or explaining why she just needed a few more minutes to read."

"You act as if Honoria weren't a child after your own heart," General Caelia said. "I seem to remember you telling me more than once how you would sneak off from your lessons to climb a tree with a copy of *Robinson Crusoe* in your pocket."

"Yes," Sir Arthur replied. "But I still climbed the tree. Books were a portal to adventure, not an end unto themselves the way they are for Honoria."

I felt an impulse to come to Miss Sherwood's defense. "She is possessed of a rare intellect. Perhaps what happens inside her head is its own sort of adventure."

Sir Arthur fixed me with an unreadable expression, but the general beamed her approval at me.

"A most perceptive observation, doctor," she said. "But on that note, I fear we must excuse ourselves. Both of us have commitments that must be seen to."

"We do?" said Sir Arthur, and again, she shot him a despairing look.

"We do," she said, standing. "And also, it might be nice for the young people to have some time themselves."

"Oh, of course," Sir Arthur said, looking abashed as he got to his feet.

"The girls should be along shortly," the general said. "I know Honoria is eager for you to meet Constancia."

"Thank you for your welcoming me into your home," I

said, standing and inclining my head. "It has been an honor and a privilege to make your acquaintance."

The general gave me one last smile, and she and Sir Arthur departed. Her prediction proved accurate, for almost as soon as they had gone, there came the sound of footsteps approaching from the other direction. As the steps got closer, there was a pause, then I heard Miss Sherwood call out, "Oh, Constancia, do come on."

"I *am* coming," replied another voice that sounded very much like Miss Sherwood's, though from further away. "These slippers are not designed for athletic exertions."

A few moments later, a side door opened, and Miss Sherwood stepped in. Even the trace of annoyance on her face could not detract from an overall air of merriness that hung about her. I knew that she had missed her sister awfully, and the reunion seemed to have restored some part of her. When she saw me, her impatience fell away entirely, and she smiled.

"Doctor," she said. "Welcome to our home. I am so glad you've come."

I barely had time to stand and make my own greetings before another figure nudged Miss Sherwood none too gently out of the way and stepped into the room. Catching sight of me, she glanced at Miss Sherwood and asked, "Is this him, then?"

I felt the oddest sense of disorientation then, taking the two women in together, because they are so alike and yet so very different. Being twins, they are identical in form and feature, but if looking upon Miss Sherwood is like gazing at a still mountain pool, Miss Constancia is a volcano. She favors clothing in that style referred to as "artistic dress", with its flowing lines and rich colors; on this occasion, she wore a garment in a deep shade of orange, topped with a crimson and purple fringed India shawl. Heavy silver bangles adorned her wrists, and her eyes had been lined with kohl. Perhaps most notably, in contrast to her sister's blonde locks, her own hair was a flaming red—presumably tinted with henna or something in that line.

Miss Sherwood looked pained for a moment by her sister's frankness, but then she shook her head and straightened her shoulders, assuming a pointedly formal tone of voice.

"Dr. Wilfred Jarvis, I would like to introduce you to my sister, Miss Constancia Sherwood." Then, turning to her sister, "Constancia, this is Dr. Jarvis."

As Miss Constancia stepped forward to offer me her hand, she openly ran her gaze up and down my form, and I felt my cheeks warm. Miss Sherwood's regard is always assessing, but there was something in Miss Constancia's attention that felt, if not exactly calculating, then at least more pointed. Miss Sherwood gathers information, parses it, files it away for future consideration, but I get the impression that Miss Constancia makes quick work of weights and measures.

"Pleased to meet you, doctor," she said as I bent over her hand. "I've heard so much about you."

"And I you," I said.

"Why don't we have a seat?" said Miss Sherwood. "I imagine tea will be along directly." I remembered then that General Caelia had ordered it, but it had never appeared. I suspected that had been by design, leaving the refreshments for "the young people".

"Do you mind if I smoke?" Miss Constancia said as we settled in, withdrawing a cigarette case from some inner dress pocket. Miss Sherwood sighed deeply.

"Constancia, please stop attempting to scandalize our guest. You never smoke at this time of day, and anyway, I have told you that those things are terrible for your health."

Miss Constancia gave her a bemused look. "So you say. Doctors claim that they are harmless, beneficial, even, for certain maladies." She turned to me, eyes bright with inquisitiveness. "What of you, Dr. Jarvis? What is your stance on the matter?"

"Well," I said, "there have been studies of the harmful effects of nicotine—"

"And besides," Miss Constancia went on, "why should it be considered scandalous? Men have smoked pipes for centuries, and nobody labels that a scandal. It is merely a form of relaxation. And what better way to spend an afternoon than in convivial fellowship accompanied by provisions that please the senses, whether that be tobacco or tea or Mrs. Morgan's heavenly custard tarts?"

As if on cue, there was a knock at the door, and a maid brought in the expected tea. Frankly, I was grateful for the reprieve. Miss Constancia's ebullience had reminded me vividly of Miss Sherwood's on the first night of our acquaintance, as well as the difficulty I'd had keeping up with her train of thought. While the substance was different, Miss Constancia was quite her equal in enthusiasm.

"This aversion to smoking is quite provincial of you, Nori," Miss Constancia continued once we all had a cup of tea in hand, though I noticed she had tucked the cigarette case back into her pocket. "Everyone smokes in town now. Dear Oscar is a great believer in tobacco's efficacy in stimulating the intellect and creative spirit. He ensures that provisions of the finest Turkish varieties are available at all of his gatherings."

"Oscar?" I said, my head swimming.

"That would be Oscar Wilde, the Irish poet and playwright who has recently begun attracting attention in

London," Miss Sherwood said, fighting a smile. "It will shock you to learn that Constancia runs with a rather bohemian set while in town."

Miss Constancia waved a dismissive hand. "Jest if you will; it is of little consequence to me. Times are changing, and it is artists leading the way with modern ideas. Just you wait—one day, I will be on the stage with my name in lights, and then we'll see who is laughing."

I nearly choked on my tea. "On the stage?" I coughed, wondering if I had heard her correctly. Miss Sherwood had mentioned that the two of them had performed in amateur theatricals, but I had assumed that was a childhood pursuit. On the contrary, Miss Constancia seemed completely sincere. She set her cup down and gave me an indulgent look.

"I know what you must be thinking. The very notion of a respectable woman treading the boards..." She pressed the back of her hand to her forehead and fell back in a faux swoon. I had to chuckle in spite of myself. "But it is a new age; there is less of a stigma now. For example, can you imagine anyone in society snubbing the Divine Sarah?" She scoffed at the very notion. Unlike Oscar, the Sarah in question did not require a surname; even a philistine such as myself has heard of Miss Bernhardt.

"But surely, she is an exception," I said, not wishing to censure her, but genuinely curious about her perspective. "No British actresses match her for praise and notoriety." She paused before answering, but she must have realized that I was asking in good faith, and she answered in kind.

"Perhaps not. But they will. And in the meantime, I will align myself with those like Oscar and Lillie, who understand the value of art for art's sake."

Once more, I was at sea. Miss Sherwood noticed and

leant in to murmur, "Lillie Langtry, former mistress of the Prince of Wales."

My eyebrows shot up, but Miss Constancia did not mark it.

"I know how you dislike being in town, Honoria, but you really ought to come with me next time. You still have not seen the new natural history museum, and I am sure you would enjoy it. Surely there is something there that you could use to write one of your papers!"

"Papers?" I said.

"Nori has been published in several journals—didn't you know?" Miss Constancia said with obvious pride. I had not, and when I glanced at Miss Sherwood for confirmation, I noticed her cheeks had gone slightly pink. It does not surprise me that she would be circumspect about such an accomplishment. While she is not shy about setting forth her reasoning, it is because she holds the truth in highest esteem, not because she wishes to draw attention to herself.

"Do come, dearest," Miss Constancia pressed. "Please?"

Miss Sherwood still looked slightly flustered, but not displeased. "I will consider it."

"Besides," Miss Constancia said. "Grandmama would love to see you. She would never say it—you know how she is—but I think she misses you dreadfully."

Miss Sherwood's eyes softened a bit at that, with affection and possibly some guilt. "I miss her as well. Perhaps I will reach out to her about meeting up in Yorkshire soon." Her gaze sharpened again as she picked up her tea. "On a related, if less agreeable, note, I have been meaning to ask —have you heard from Cal since you've been back?"

Miss Constancia snorted. "I am shocked that you would even pose such a ridiculous question."

"Who is Cal?" I said. I had leant in toward Miss Sherwood and hoped I was speaking in a confidential manner, but it was Miss Constancia who answered.

"Our brother."

I blinked at her. While Miss Sherwood had spoken of her sister often, I had never heard of this other sibling. Miss Sherwood, noticing my confusion, took pity on me.

"Calidore is our half-brother," she said. "From Mama's first marriage."

I looked at her then. Miss Constancia had communicated a marked air of disdain in her description, while Miss Sherwood's voice was even more level than usual— flat, even.

"I don't recall you mentioning him," I said.

"Until only recently, he has resided in the Home Lands," she said, referring to that ancestral domain of the Folk that is verboten to outsiders. "We are... not close."

I felt that there was a story there, but it seemed unwise to pursue it in that moment. The introduction of this mysterious brother had cast a pall on the conversation, which had been so amiable only moments before. Eager to restore the mood, I thought of the message in my jacket and decided now might be a good time to deploy it.

"Oh," I said, taking it out. "I have a message for you. From Waddington."

Miss Sherwood's eyes went wide. "*Waddington?*"

I nodded and passed her the envelope.

"Waddington," Miss Constancia said thoughtfully as Miss Sherwood opened the letter. "Isn't he the disagreeable one who is too handsome for his own good?"

"He is," Miss Sherwood said distractedly, scanning the lines on the page. "This says there is a delicate matter that he thinks would benefit from my counsel."

"Hang on," I said, nonplussed. "He is asking you for *help*? After the way he behaved during the Drebber affair?"

"It seems so, yes," she said, folding the letter and returning it to the envelope. "He has requested that I meet with him and an unnamed associate at his cottage tonight. Chaperoned, of course, but he asked that I select my company with care, as the matter requires the utmost discretion."

"What in God's name is he up to?" I said, but she only shrugged.

"I do not know. He gave no specifics, was in fact careful to use only the vaguest generalities."

"Ooh," Miss Constancia drawled. "How delightfully cryptic."

"I shall ask Mary to accompany me," said Miss Sherwood. As Miss Sherwood's lady's maid, Mary made an acceptable chaperone, though I suspected it was Mary's perceptive and strategic mind that had truly inspired her mistress's choice. "Would you also be willing to join us, doctor?"

"Of course," I said, smiling. "Even if my curiosity hadn't been piqued, it is only next door."

"Why does Mary get to go?" cut in Miss Constancia. "My curiosity has been piqued as well. Perhaps I wanted to be your chaperone for the evening."

Miss Sherwood held the letter up with two fingers. "Discretion, dear sister. It is not your strong suit."

Miss Constancia put on an offended expression, but after a moment, she did murmur, "Fair enough."

That settled, I departed, left to my own devices until the appointed time. As I made my way home, I began plotting what I would say to Mrs. Howell once I arrived. I would need to pay her for the day, of course; I had, after all, left her there in the house rather than sending her away with a firm refusal. But there was no question of her remaining on. I am practiced at being self-sufficient. I do not need someone following around after me, making a fuss over trivialities.

When I walked into the house, however, I found not only that Mrs. Howell had already departed, but that she had also left a note demanding that I give her a key the next day so that she could come and go freely. I crumpled the note into a tight ball and threw it into the wastebasket, but then I realized something—I felt more comfortable in the house than I had in my entire time on the island. Mrs. Howell had scrubbed and dusted everything; if I wasn't mistaken, she had also aired out the entire ground floor. There was even a bowl of fresh flowers on the table. She had, in short, done a marvelous job of making my standard-issue cottage feel like a home.

In the space of two minutes, I had gone from not wanting anything to do with her to thinking maybe it wouldn't be so bad to have a housekeeper after all. This left me feeling rather annoyed—at Mrs. Howell, at whoever had sent her, and, perhaps most of all, at myself—so I set about making a simple supper in my frustratingly immaculate kitchen and waited to meet Miss Sherwood.

It was already dark when I made the brief walk to Waddington's cottage. There is not a proper lane in front of our little group of dwellings that would accommodate a carriage, but in short order, I saw Miss Sherwood and Mary making their way across the lawn from the high street. It was quiet in our section of the British Quarter, with only the wind in the trees making noise, but even so, I could not hear the women's footsteps until they were practically upon me; the new grass was already thick enough to mute their treads. When they reached the path, we exchanged brief greetings, and I knocked on the door, perhaps more eager than I'd realized to discover what had made Waddington so evasive.

Waddington himself answered the door, ushering us into a surprisingly tasteful and orderly parlor. As he had intimated in his note, the room boasted another occupant, a neat and finely dressed man with a mustache and a full head of graying hair. He had been staring into the depths of a whiskey tumbler but looked up when he heard us enter. Even if he had not done so, I would have recognized him. After all, I encountered him regularly in the course of my work. It was Lord Marsden, the British secretary ambassador to Ynis Witrin.

As I tried to contain my shock, Waddington spoke up from behind us.

"Dr. Jarvis, Miss Sherwood—I believe you know my uncle."

Chapter 2

21 May 1881, cont.

IN LIGHT OF THIS REVELATION, Miss Sherwood remained coolly perceptive, as is her wont, but I found myself struggling to do the same. In a flash, I remembered both Waddington and Pryce alluding to family connections that had played a role in Waddington being stationed on Ynis Witrin but realized no one had ever really clarified what those connections were. Now I had my answer.

At Miss Sherwood's entrance, Lord Marsden had gotten to his feet and given her a brief bow.

"Miss Sherwood," he said. "It is lovely to see you again."

Miss Sherwood inclined her head, and Waddington gestured for us to be seated. Miss Sherwood and I joined Lord Marsden near the hearth while Mary, owing to her status as a servant, even one employed in the role of chaperone, selected a chair tucked away in the corner.

Waddington offered tea, which we all refused, then took his own seat.

"Thank you for coming," Lord Marsden said to Miss Sherwood, and in the firelight, I could see that he looked more haggard than usual. "I find that I am in a spot of trouble, and Jacob tells me your counsel was of great help in the Drebber affair."

Where Miss Sherwood had seemed unruffled at Lord Marsden's presence and his heretofore unknown connection to Waddington, this statement clearly caught her off guard. I do not believe the others noticed—I was only able to, I think, because I have begun to learn her mannerisms —but she flicked a quick, questioning glance at Waddington before addressing the secretary ambassador.

"I am happy to hear it, my lord," she said. "I did my best in that instance to pursue justice and maintain the peace between our peoples."

Lord Marsden nodded. "I am happy to hear *that*. And I hope you will be willing to put your talents to work again." Instantly, I was reminded of Pryce's complaint earlier that afternoon—a conflict between the castle and the secretary ambassador's office. Could that issue and this be connected?

Lord Marsden rose and went to the fireplace, gazing into the flames for a moment before turning to address us once more.

"As you may be aware," said Lord Marsden. "Princess Beatrice will be in attendance at the ball celebrating Her Majesty's birthday."

I wasn't entirely sure how he thought we wouldn't be aware of the princess's imminent arrival, but I refrained from saying so out loud.

"As is tradition, Her Royal Highness is meant to pay tribute to the bond between the Seelie Court and the

Empire by wearing the Iris Circlet at the ball." He paused and retrieved a slim book from a nearby occasional table. "Do you know of the Iris Circlet?"

Ah. So this was the "bauble" Pryce had referred to, in a masterpiece of understatement. After Miss Sherwood and I nodded to indicate we were familiar with the legendary piece, Lord Marsden passed the book to Miss Sherwood. She opened to a detailed color engraving marked with a ribbon, and I peeked over her shoulder.

The circlet in the picture was true to its namesake, that Greek goddess who personified the rainbow, and surpassed any description of it I had ever heard. It was composed of twining cords of silver and gold, within which, according to the accompanying text, were set thirty-nine stones, all sapphires that had traveled to the British Isles via the Silk Road in the sixth century. Some were the customary blue, while others came in shades of yellow, green, and purple. In the center was a particularly impressive specimen that was, at least in the rendering, an exquisite shade balanced somewhere between orange and pink; according to the text, it was a rare variety called padparadscha, native to Sri Lanka and considered very precious. The piece was indeed a worthy symbol of unity —the stones provided by King Arthur to the Seelie Court as a gift, then gifted back to him in the stunning example of Folk work.

"You'll remember, of course," said Lord Marsden, "that upon the Folk's return from self-imposed exile, the prince regent offered the circlet to Queen Mab as an acknowledgment of the renewed alliance between our nations. Ever since, it has been brought out whenever a female representative of the British royal family has visited the island for a state occasion."

"That is fascinating," said Miss Sherwood, with her

customary directness. "But what does it have to do with your summons?"

Lord Marsden sighed and sank into his chair once more. "For reasons that were never made entirely clear to me, I became the one responsible for taking charge of the circlet this year. It seemed like just one more hassle, so I thought to get the task out of the way before preparations for the ball began in earnest. I contacted my counterpart at the castle and requested that the circlet be delivered to the embassy, where it would remain until the princess's arrival. The task was accomplished, and everything seemed to be going well—until last night."

He paused, infuriatingly like a music hall performer holding back a line delivery to keep an audience in suspense, but my impatience was somewhat assuaged when I saw how he was struggling to get the next words out of his mouth. Waddington took a step forward from where he stood in the corner.

"Uncle," he said, in perhaps the most compassionate tone I'd even heard him use. "Tell them."

Lord Marsden slumped, and I thought his face turned a bit grey, but finally he said, "I had worried that the circlet was not secure enough in the embassy offices. I thought if I brought it home with me, and stored it in my personal office safe, I would be better able to keep an eye on it, but that was all folly. Because now, some of its stones have disappeared."

"Disappeared?" I burst out. "But how?"

"We don't know," said Waddington. "That is why we requested Miss Sherwood's assistance."

There was a rather tense moment of silence, but then Miss Sherwood withdrew a notebook and pen from her reticule and lifted her chin.

"Very well," she said. "Let us establish a picture of

what has happened. Tell me about your household, Lord Marsden."

He resumed his seat, looking thoughtful. "There is our housekeeper, of course, and my valet. They have been with me for years, and I trust them implicitly. There are a couple of other servants, a stableboy and a house maid, but they both live in Glastonbury; they can be set aside altogether. And then there is Lucy—she is the kitchen maid and has only been in our service for a few months. She came with excellent references and has done good work for us, but..."

Miss Sherwood waited a beat, then urged him to continue. "Has there been anything about her performance that has struck you as noteworthy? Or bothersome?"

Lord Marsden pursed his lips. "Well, she is a very pretty girl, you see, and so there are sometimes rather useless fellows lingering about the house to speak to her. But we shall get to that."

Miss Sherwood glanced up from her jotting, but she did not invite him to elaborate. "And what of your family?"

"You know Lady Marsden, of course. And there is Clara."

"Your daughter?"

"Niece, technically," he clarified. "But when my brother died five years ago and left her alone in the world, I adopted her and have looked upon her ever since as my daughter." His expression brightened for a moment. "She is the light of our home—quiet and gentle, but also intelligent and capable. She has become indispensable to us, helping to run the household while Lady Marsden is occupied with social obligations and often serving as a secretary to me when I work at home rather than the office." Once more, his face became somber. "It has been a blessing to have such a lovely child, after the pains that we have taken over our son."

"Your son?" said Miss Sherwood.

Marsden nodded. "Edward. He is a bright boy, but headstrong and impulsive. Perhaps we have overindulged him, but even as a child, he ran wild, heedless of any consequences." His gaze moved to Waddington. "The two of you were peas in a pod." His expression was such a profound mixture of fondness and disappointment that I felt like a voyeur seeing it. Waddington shifted again, and his eyes dropped to the floor, but he said nothing.

"And he has retained these habits into adulthood?" Miss Sherwood prompted gently.

Lord Marsden cleared his throat, returning from his reverie. "He has. I have striven to involve him in the running of the estate, but in vain. In truth, he is a disaster with money. From his earliest days in society, he has gravitated to those with long purses and expensive habits. He's often turned to gambling in his efforts to keep up, and in this area, he is perhaps the unluckiest fellow alive. He has come to me again and again for advances on his allowance, then outright 'loans' that we both know he is never going to pay back. I was at my wit's end, but recently, he seemed to be improving, largely due to the influence of his friend Sir George Brumwell."

From the corner of my eye, I saw Waddington's head snap up, his gaze intent. I could not tell if this action fell within Miss Sherwood's field of vision, but I did notice a shift in her posture at the same moment—a straightening of her spine that was slight but spoke of alertness.

"Can you tell me a little of this Sir George?" Miss Sherwood said.

"My son has known him since they were boys—Jacob, too." He looked at Waddington who nodded in confirmation, face grim. "As far as I knew they were never particularly close, but lately, Edward has been seeing more of him. I have always thought Sir George a fine young man—so enterprising and refined. Edward's character is very much improved since taking up a more intimate friendship. He still resides in town but has taken an increased interest in assuming his duties as heir. He has begun visiting more often, often bringing Sir George with him. He had even seemed to be taking steps to present his suit to Clara once more, with possible expectation of success."

Miss Sherwood raised her eyebrows. "Edward wishes to marry his cousin?"

"He does," Lord Marsden confirmed. "He adores her, always has. It has long been the great wish of my heart as well, for them to be wed, for I believe he would benefit from her influence. He first proposed, oh, it must be three years ago now. And she refused him. I could hardly blame her, considering his dissolute ways, but his new demonstrations of responsibility had given me hope that such a thing might be achieved." He sighed. "And it is all over now. All over."

"What makes you say so, my lord?" said Miss Sherwood.

Lord Marsden sank lower in his chair, and when he spoke again, his voice was more subdued.

"After dinner, we took coffee in the sitting room. Lucy had brought in the tray, and I thought she had closed the door behind her, but now... now I cannot say for sure.

"I was explaining to the family how the circlet had come into my care and how I had brought it home to insure its safety. Edward asked what I had done with it, and when I told him I placed it in the safe, he laughed. 'What, that old thing?' he said. 'I used to dip in there all the time, just for a laugh.'"

"He knew of the safe?"

Lord Marsden nodded. "It was in the library at our country estate in his youth. I had it moved here when we took up residence."

"And his words didn't alarm you?"

"No," said Lord Marsden. "He is forever making ludicrous assertions, just to provoke reactions, has done since he was a boy. We had hoped he'd grow out of it, to no avail. And it seemed impossible that he knew the combination—only Lady Marsden and I know it, and I have made a point never to write it down."

"So what happened next that you believe led to the stones' disappearance?" said Miss Sherwood.

Lord Marsden's lips settled into a grim line. "Later that night, Edward came to me in my office."

"And this is the office where the safe is kept?" Miss Sherwood interjected, still scribbling in her notebook.

"Yes," said Lord Marsden. "It is on the ground floor, next to our bedroom."

"And what did he wish to speak to you about?"

Lord Marsden sighed. "He asked me for money. Again."

At this, Miss Sherwood put down her pencil, giving him a look of sympathy. "That must have disappointed you."

"It did," Lord Marsden agreed. "Especially after a long stretch of what I'd thought was sterling conduct. He requested £200. When I asked what it was for, he became evasive and pleading, presenting me with a host of terrible consequences that would befall him if he was not able to cover this last debt. He swore up and down that he was done with gambling for good, but I found that after everything he's done, I simply couldn't believe him. I shouted at him, told him I had already been far too generous with him. Then words were exchanged on both sides that I am hesitant to repeat." He paused, looking regretful, and tears shone in his eyes. "Eventually, he stormed out, leaving me there to stew."

"I stayed in the office for a while after that—I confess that I took a bit of brandy to calm my nerves. But eventually, the time came for me to retire. I thought I might feel more settled if I checked the security of the house before I went to bed, even though Clara is usually the one to perform that duty, once the servants have left for the night. As I made a circuit of the lower floor, I came across Mary herself at one of the windows, having already begun her usual task, and I watched her test the lock on the window as I approached.

"'She turned to me with a strange expression on her face and asked, 'Uncle, did you give Lucy permission to go out tonight?' I had done no such thing, and I told her so. Then she said, 'I just saw her come in through the kitchen door. I think she was down by the side gate talking to someone, and I can't think of any good that would come of such an arrangement.'

"Well, I would not have questioned that assertion on a normal day, but considering the events of the evening, I was mightily distressed. In fact, I was ready to go rouse Lucy and get to the bottom of things, but Clara soothed me and convinced me the conversation could wait until the morning. She kissed me goodnight, and I completed my errand and, satisfied, went to bed."

"If all seemed well when you retired, how did you come to suspect that something was wrong?" asked Miss Sherwood.

Lord Marsden sighed and ran a hand over his face. "I am not a very heavy sleeper at the best of times, and my anxiety over the situation no doubt made me even less disposed to rest than usual. About two in the morning, I was roused by a sound somewhere in the house—something like a window being closed. All was silent again by the time I came fully awake, but I couldn't put the notion of it out of my head. I lay there listening hard, and after a moment, I heard the faint sound of footsteps in the next room. Shaking, I slipped out of bed and went to the office door, peeking carefully around the edge.

"The gas was half up, just as I had left it, and Edward, dressed only in his shirt and trousers, was standing there, holding the circlet and wrenching at it with all his strength. I cried out, and he whirled to face me, dropping it in his surprise. I snatched the piece up and examined it, only to find that one of the gold corners, together with three stones, was gone.

"I confess that I rather lost my head. I shouted at him, calling him a villain and a thief. I demanded that he produce the missing stones. He swore none were missing, and when I pointed to the broken area, he went white in the face. He swore to me that he hadn't done anything with them, that he was entirely innocent, but of course, I did not believe him. After our argument, it was clear to me that he had decided to take the jewels as recompense.

"When I told him so, his demeanor shifted from contrite to hostile. He claimed I was treating him abominably, that he would never treat a son the way I had treated him, and that he was washing his hands of the whole business.

"In the middle of all this, Lady Marsden had rushed in with Clara on her heels, both of them having been roused by the clamor of our voices. Clara took one look at the circlet and Edward's anguished face and fainted dead away. I left off arguing to check on her, together with my wife, while Edward stood there watching us.

"The sight of his cousin so affected seemed to sober him up. He made an effort to collect himself as Lady Marsden called out for smelling salts, then asked if I might allow him to leave for the space of five minutes, that he could perhaps bring this situation to a happy resolution. I laughed and said that I would not give him cover to further conceal his crimes, and that I would instead call the constabulary in to take him into custody. He went oddly still when I said that, all the fight draining out of him, and when he spoke, his voice was calm and even.

"'No, you won't,' he said. 'If word of the theft got out, it could cause a scandal of the highest order. What would Lord Evrain and his minions make of such a blunder on the embassy's part? They'd be after the queen to expel the British before you could blink.'" We all glanced at each other, recognizing the truth in the assertion. "'Whatever happens with an investigation, whoever may be uncovered as the perpetrator, the responsibility will rest on your shoulders, because the circlet was in your care. And I don't think you are willing to be the engineer of your own destruction.' And God forgive me, he was right. He was right." Lord Marsden dropped his head into his hands.

"What happened then?" prompted Miss Sherwood.

Lord Marsden straightened. "I was so angry at his continued refusal to confess to what he'd done that I ran to his room and began tearing it apart, certain I would find the jewels. He came to the door and just stood there watching, that same eerie look of calm on his face. Eventually, I ran out of places to look and stood panting among the wreckage. Edward only said that he would not be my concern any longer, as he intended to leave in the morning. Then he took me by the arm, steered me into the hallway, and slammed the door in my face."

"What did you do?" said Miss Sherwood.

"I retired to my bedroom and tried to regain control of my emotions. I only meant to calm myself, then attempt once more to have a rational discussion with him, but the excitement caught up with me, and I slipped into a doze before the fire. When I woke and realized what had happened, I went straight to Edward's room, but he had already departed."

"And you haven't heard from him since?"

"I have not."

Miss Sherwood stared down at her notes, tapping her pencil against the paper a few times, before continuing. "Do you receive much company, Lord Marsden?"

"Not so much," he said. "Lady Marsden and I attend quite a few events in the evening, of course, but we rarely receive visitors beyond the demands of my position."

"I do not believe I have seen Clara in a social context. Does she not go out with you?"

"Not generally, no. She does not care much for society."

Miss Sherwood raised an eyebrow. "Is that not unusual for a young girl?"

Lord Marsden straightened, and when he spoke again, his voice had a defensive note. "She is of a quiet nature and prefers to keep her own company; even when we have encouraged her, she has resisted. Besides, she is not so very young. She is past twenty now."

"This episode, from what you say, seems to have been a shock to her as well."

He sighed. "Oh, definitely. Out of all of us, she seems the most affected. She has not ceased weeping since the incident occurred. We have been most concerned about her well-being."

"Does she share your opinion of your son's guilt?"

"No. She has, in fact, asserted his innocence from the

very beginning and never wavered in her stance. But that is just her tender heart speaking. Normally, that sweetness of temper is to her credit, but I fear it has led her astray here. How could it be otherwise when we all saw him with the circlet in his hands?"

"That proof may not be the conclusive as you believe," said Miss Sherwood, mollifying. "Was the remainder of the circlet damaged?"

"Yes, it was twisted."

"And you did not think it possible that he might have been trying to straighten it?"

Lord Marsden's face softened. "Bless you, child. You are like Clara, trying to find a silver lining behind this terrible cloud. I appreciate your kindness. But it is too heavy a task. What was Edward doing there at all? If his purpose was innocent, why not just say so?"

"My stance has nothing to do with kindness, my lord," said Miss Sherwood, sounding miffed at the very suggestion. "His silence appears to me to cut both ways. If he were guilty, why did he not simply lie?"

Lord Marsden sat back, looking perplexed, but also a bit hopeful. "I do not know."

"Have you looked for the gems anywhere besides your office and your son's chamber?"

"Well... no."

Miss Sherwood sighed. "My lord, I believe this case strikes rather deeper than you were at first inclined to think. You say that it appeared to you to be a simple case, but I am finding it exceedingly complex. Consider the theory you have proposed. You claim that your son came down from his bed, went to your office at great risk to himself, opened the safe, took out your circlet, broke off a portion of it with his bare hands, went off to some other place, concealed the missing gems, and then returned with the circlet, thereby exposing himself to the greatest danger of being discovered."

"I suppose it does sound far-fetched when you lay it out like that," Lord Marsden said. "But what other theory is there? If his motives were innocent, why did he not explain them?"

"I do not know," confessed Miss Sherwood. "But I believe I can find out if I am permitted to visit your house on the morrow."

Lord Marsden nodded, and arrangements were made for a call the following morning, then we made our farewells and left. Once on the path outside Waddington's cottage, Miss Sherwood, Mary, and I paused to take stock.

"I did not realize you were in the habit of taking notes during interviews," I said, nodding towards her reticule.

"I am not. But it tends to make people nervous when I simply gaze at them as they speak." Her manner turned thoughtful. "I must admit that was not at all what I expected when I left the house this evening."

"Do you really believe the son to be innocent?" I asked.

She nodded. "I will need to conduct a detailed investigation, of course, but based on the information we have been given thus far, he does not make sense to me as a suspect."

"Who leaps out at you then?" I said. "What about this maid, Lucy?"

"I know Lucy," said Mary. "She is a decent sort—doesn't seem likely to get caught up in anything like this."

"We do not deal in 'likely', Mary," said Miss Sherwood, and Mary sighed.

"I know, I know. When you have excluded the impossible, whatever remains, however improbable, must be the truth." This last was conveyed in the harried sing-song of an oft-repeated maxim, and Miss Sherwood smiled crookedly. I found it uncommonly charming.

"Well, whatever it is that happened," I said, "I am sure you will sort it out in a trice."

"Yes, of course," Miss Sherwood said, but there seemed to be a touch less certainty in her voice than usual. I wondered on it, but just then the breeze picked up; for all that it is May, it still gets chilly at night, and the wind was quite brisk. Miss Sherwood huddled more deeply into her cloak, and I took this as my sign to escort her and Mary to the carriage that waited to take them back to the castle.

Now the hour is late, and I plan to sit down for what has become my customary nightly reading and then see myself off to bed. I was very pleased to receive the latest Wilkie Collins that you sent, dear sister. I dispatched a short note to that effect right away, but I am including the sentiment in this account as well, so when I share this journal with you at the conclusion of my service here, you may once more feel the warmth of my gratitude. I do not find Collins's more recent work equal to *The Moonstone* or *The Woman in White*, but there is still a comforting famil-iarity to it. Plus, we will have a mystery of our own to tackle in the morning—perhaps I can learn a thing or two.

Your brother,
Wilf

Chapter 3

22 May 1881

DEAR ESTHER–

The next morning, Waddington and I met at the office according to plan. It was more or less a normal morning for me, but Waddington was up much earlier than is typical and, thus, in a bad temper. For his part, Pryce was so busy that he did not seem to take any note of Waddington's unusual punctuality, nor did he argue when I told him we were stepping out for an unspecified errand. I wasn't sure how much he really knew about the situation, so I figured the less said about it, the better.

Together, Waddington and I proceeded to the secretary ambassador's residence, a large, comfortable place further out along our end of the Quarter, where the buildings are not so tightly packed and the character of the neighborhood begins to favor aesthetics over utility. The house faced the high street but was set back enough to accommodate a modest lawn and a path lined with ornamental trees and flowers. A track for deliveries curved around the side of the lawn to the back of the house, where a few stately oaks peeked up over the roofline, and I caught a glimpse of a stone wall that divided the property from a paved lane behind it that led to other houses and outbuildings.

As the two of us approached the front door, I caught sight of Mary peering off towards the side of the house, though what specifically she was looking at, I could not say.

"Good morning, Mary," I called as we approached, and she turned and bobbed a quick curtsy.

"Good morning, doctor, lieutenant." As we each nodded in acknowledgment, I wondered at her presence and felt an odd sinking sensation at the prospect that had been sent in Miss Sherwood's stead.

"Have you a message for us from your mistress?"

"Oh, no," Mary said. "She is here. She only stepped around that corner of the house there, looking for anything that might help with the investigation."

Just as she finished this explanation, there was a rustle in a nearby shrubbery, and then Miss Sherwood was picking her way through the flower beds to join us on the path. She wore a very fashionable visiting ensemble in shades of blue and green with a matching hat, though upon closer inspection I thought I saw walking boots peeking out from beneath her skirt, and I realized that the green skirt was a strategic choice, meant to hide potential grass stains acquired tramping through underbrush. There was a flush on her cheeks from exertion and the cool breeze, and she smiled with exceptional good humor.

"Good morning, gentlemen," she said, ostensibly including Waddington in the greeting, but not deigning to look at him. "I took the opportunity provided by your tardiness to conduct an assessment of the grounds. But now that you have arrived, we can begin our visitation proper."

"We arrived precisely at the appointed time," Waddington protested, but Miss Sherwood had already moved on from the conversation. She stepped up to the door and knocked soundly.

Her summons was answered by a timid human maid who ushered us in, took our hats, and escorted us to the drawing room. There were chairs clustered around a low table where a tea service had already been set out for us. Miss Sherwood took one of these, while Mary again took a discreet seat off to one side. Waddington and I went to stand by the hearth, where a fire was blazing cheerily.

We had only been there a few minutes when Lord Marsden appeared, greeting us enthusiastically, despite his careworn appearance. The maid was just passing around tea when another woman entered the room. She was rather tall and slim, with dark hair and eyes. Her face, in contrast, was pale and wan, at least where it was not red from weeping. She went directly to Lord Marsden, laying her hand on his arm and addressing him as if the two of them were alone in the room.

"Uncle, have you received any word from Edward?"

Lord Marsden patted her hand consolingly. "I have not, my dear."

"But we must find him!" she exclaimed. "He is all alone, and he was so angry when he left —what if he does himself an injury?"

Gently, Lord Marsden led her to a chair and bade her sit. "I am as anxious to find him as you are, my dear, and to get to the bottom of this whole sorry business. In fact, I have engaged an investigator to that very end."

Her eyes scanned the room, eventually landing on me. "This gentleman?" she said to her uncle.

"No," he said. "It is the lady—Miss Sherwood. Jacob tells me that she is quite resourceful and was a great help in a recent matter at the attaché's office."

Miss Holder's shocked gaze turned to the lady in question.

"Miss Sherwood, this is my niece, Miss Clara Holder," said Lord Marsden

Miss Sherwood extended her hand. "How do you do, Miss Holder?"

Miss Holder gave Miss Sherwood's hand a perfunctory shake, but immediately turned back to her uncle. "But I don't see why this is necessary. This has all been a big misunderstanding. I'm sure that if you could get Edward to come home and the two of you could discuss the situation calmly, everything would be set to rights."

"Oh, my dear," Lord Marsden said, looking at her sadly. "I think we are past that at this point."

Miss Holder stared at him for a long moment, then looked away and took up the tea that had been set out for her on the table. She was trying to put on a brave face, but I could see her lip trembling.

After several seconds of awkward silence, Miss Sherwood slid nearer to Miss Holder and addressed her in a soft, confiding way.

"Miss Holder, would it make you feel any better to know that, based on what your uncle has told us, I do not believe your cousin to be guilty?"

Miss Holder looked up at her with wet eyes. "You don't?"

"No," said Miss Sherwood with a reassuring smile.

"It is, of course, too soon to make that judgment definitively," Lord Marsden said, and Miss Sherwood shot him such a look that he, peer of the realm and secretary ambassador of the Crown, hung his head like a chided schoolboy.

Turning her attention back to Miss Holder, Miss Sherwood said. "I am here to gather evidence of what happened that night. If your cousin is indeed innocent, he has nothing to fear."

Miss Holder took a shaky breath and sat her cup down again.

"May I ask you some questions?" Miss Sherwood said.

"I suppose," said Miss Holder, sounding not at all sure, but she lifted her chin and awaited Miss Sherwood's inquiries.

"Your uncle said he was awakened by a sound in the house last night. Did you hear anything?"

"Nothing," Miss Holder said. "That is, until Uncle began shouting. I came out when I heard that."

"Your Uncle tells us you typically secure the house at night. Did you lock all the windows on the night of the theft?"

"Yes."

"And all of them were locked when you woke?"

"Yes."

"We were led to understand that one of the maids of the house has some admirers. Your uncle says you told him that she had been out to see one of them that night?"

"Yes," said Miss Holder. "And it was she who had waited on us in the drawing room and may have heard uncle's remarks about the circlet."

"Ah," said Miss Sherwood. "So you believe that she went out to tell her lover, and that the two of them planned the robbery."

"But what is the good of all these vague theories," cried Lord Marsden, "when I have told you that I saw Edward with the circlet in his hands!?"

"Uncle—" Waddington began, but Miss Sherwood held up a hand to stop him. "Now, Miss Holder, about this maid—Lucy is her name, correct?" Miss Holder nodded. "You say that you saw her return to the house through the kitchen door?"

Miss Holder nodded again. "Yes. When I went to see if the door was locked for the night, she was just slipping inside. I saw the man, too, over her shoulder."

"Do you know him?"

"Oh, yes. He is the green-grocer who brings vegetables to the house."

"He stood to the left of the door?" Miss Sherwood said, sketching the scene in the air with her hands. "Farther up the path than is necessary to reach the door?"

"Yes."

"And he is a man with a wooden leg?"

Miss Holder's eyes went wide with amazement and, if I wasn't mistaken, a little fear.

"But you are like one of those mind readers who go on stage! How do you know that?" She smiled, but it was brittle.

"Oh, I think you'll find I prove less of a charlatan than those fellows," Miss Sherwood said, with a thin smile of her own and an unreadable expression in her eye. "There is no flimflam to my theorizing—only observation and deduction."

"I see," said Miss Holder, and she sipped her tea.

"On that note," Miss Sherwood said "Your uncle has already given us his account of events on the night of the robbery. Would you be willing to verify some of his observations for me?"

Miss Holder nodded once, looking tense. Miss Sherwood walked her through Lord Marsden's story of the night, pausing every so often to ask Miss Holder for conformation on some point or other, which the lady provided in curt monosyllables. As the tale came to its end, Miss Sherwood looked up, addressing uncle and niece.

"One last thing," she said. "Edward had no shoes or slippers on when you saw him, is that correct?"

For a moment, neither spoke, only sat blinking at her, but eventually, Lord Marsden broke the silence. "He had nothing on, save his trousers and shirt." He glanced at Miss Holder, who nodded in agreement. Miss Sherwood gave a brisk nod of her own and tucked her notebook back into her reticule.

"I think I should like to take a look around the house, if that is all right."

Lord Marsden nodded, and Miss Sherwood rose and left the room. Those of us left behind kept up a stream of polite conversation, but I could tell that Miss Holder was still unsettled in mind. After a few minutes, she stood and, claiming a headache, excused herself for a rest. I continued speaking with Lord Marsden and Waddington, but I did wonder where she had gone. I had begun concocting a reason to leave drawing room, so that I might do a little investigating of my own, when Lord Marsden brought the conversation back around to Miss Sherwood.

"Jacob tells me that you worked closely with Miss Sherwood on that affair earlier in the spring."

I felt my hackles rise, driven once more by some implacable instinct to protect Miss Sherwood from any hint of aspersion or slander, but Lord Marsden seemed merely curious. This, I was coming to realize, was a common enough response to my, well... I suppose my partnership with Miss Sherwood. Part of the fascination was, of course, due to her sex, as it remains unusual for a young lady to pursue the occupations that engage Miss Sherwood. But even aside from that, I imagine we do make an odd pairing, with our differing backgrounds and positions in life. However, I also find that I am less and less concerned with what other people think.

"I did, after a fashion," I replied.

"And you really believe that she can resolve this situation? It has left me feeling most wretched; I admit that in some moments, I am given over to despondency. And she seems so young and..." He did not finish, but I had a feeling I knew what he meant. Sheltered. Untested. *Female.*

I straightened in my seat. "I assure you, my lord, that I have the utmost confidence in Miss Sherwood's abilities. If anyone is able to see this through, it will be her."

He looked at me for a long moment and nodded. I glanced at Waddington, poised to rebuff any disparaging remarks of his pertaining to Miss Sherwood, but he remained silent. I was still puzzling over this newfound reticence of his when Miss Sherwood returned. Lord Marsden leapt to his feet at the sight of her.

"Did you find anything of note, Miss Sherwood?"

"Hard to tell," she said. "I will need time to revisit and synthesize the evidence. But I was wondering if I might see the circlet. Do you still have it in your possession?"

"I do," said Lord Marsden. "Give me but a moment, and I will retrieve it for you."

He departed, giving Miss Sherwood an opportunity to take her own tea. Presently, he returned with a leather case. Placing it on the tea table, he opened it, revealing the circlet resting on a bed of velvet. It truly was a beautiful piece of work, inspired, like most Folk work, by the graceful organic lines of nature, and the stones were even more breathtaking and vibrant than they had appeared in the engraving. That made it all the more dreadful to see the broken spot in the metalwork where the missing stones had been set.

"Here you are," Lord Marsden said and stepped back from the table. Miss Sherwood leant forward and picked up the circlet, turning it to and fro in her hands to get a good sense of it. Finally, she held it out to Lord Marsden.

"I see there is a corner here which corresponds to that which has been so unfortunately lost." She pointed to the undamaged side of the circlet. "Might I beg of you to break it off?"

Lord Marsden recoiled. "Are you mad? What at all has that to do with finding the missing sapphires?"

Miss Sherwood was serene. "Am I to understand then, that you are not willing to undertake the task?"

"I wouldn't dream of it!"

With a nod, Miss Sherwood turned to me. "Doctor, may I impose upon you to do the honors?"

I confess that the request gave me some pause. Setting aside the fact that the circlet was a priceless treasure, it was a symbol of the long history that bound our nations together. Breaking it, especially at a time when that bond was tenuous, seemed an affront to everything we were trying to do on the island. But the reality was that both the circlet and the comity between our people was already fractured; there was only so much more harm that I could do. Plus, I knew Miss Sherwood well enough now to know that she wouldn't propose such an action without good reason.

I extended my hand, and she placed the circlet into it. Taking hold of the piece at its undamaged end and its center, I took a deep breath and did my best to break it in two.

"Well?" said Miss Sherwood after a rather anticlimactic moment.

"I feel it give a little," I said, straining with the continued application of my strength to the circlet and the resulting twinge in my bad shoulder, "but I think it would take some time to wrench it enough to get the stones out, let alone snap the metal." I released my grip with a huff.

Miss Sherwood turned to Lord Marsden. "Do you see? Dr. Jarvis is a soldier and possessed of greater strength and dexterity than the average man." I felt a surprising flush of pleasure at these words but did my best to school my features as I passed the circlet back to her. "Based on what you have told us of your son, I find it unlikely that he could have broken the piece with only brute strength, but let's suppose he had. There would have been a noise like a pistol shot. Don't you think that would have attracted your notice if you were only in the next room?"

Lord Marsden crumpled into a chair, resting his head on a fist.

"I do not know what to think. It is all dark to me."

Miss Sherwood resumed her seat, gazing at Lord Marsden intently.

"Tell me, sir," she said. "What would you give to see the gems returned?"

"Everything!" he cried. "My entire fortune!"

She smiled indulgently. "I do not think that will be necessary. But in terms of market value, what price do you think stones of that quality might command? £800 each? A thousand?"

I went a bit light in the head at the mention of such an amount, but Lord Marsden only became serious, considering.

"I believe a thousand per stone would not be outside the realm of possibility."

"Would you be willing to issue me a cheque for that amount, to be returned to you if the gems are not recovered?"

At this, Lord Marsden tipped over into astonishment,

as well he might. He looked to Waddington, and I felt certain Miss Sherwood's stratagem to come to nothing, but to my great surprise, Waddington nodded. As Lord Marsden proceeded to his desk and withdrew his cheque-book, Miss Sherwood caught Waddington's eye and tipped hear head in grateful acknowledgment. Apparently having reached his threshold of virtuous behavior, Waddington merely sniffed and looked away.

"I would never have believed I'd be willing to do something such as this," Lord Marsden muttered as he wrote. "But desperate times…"

He finished and handed the cheque to Miss Sherwood, who slipped in into her reticule and stood. As she neared the door, she turned back to Lord Marsden.

"I know it is difficult, my lord," she said gently, "but try not to allow yourself to be overtaken by despair. We have more to work with than you might realize. This crisis may yet be averted."

It was not the first time I had seen Miss Sherwood display this sort of compassion to a person is distress, but it was touching nonetheless, a reminder that however much she relished the intellectual challenge of a problem, she was truly driven by an impulse to help those in need. For his part, Lord Marsden smiled politely but looked far from convinced.

Waddington saw us out. At the door, he asked me to make his excuses to Pryce, feeling that he needed to stay on the house, and we made plans to reconvene in the morning for an update.

"The clock is ticking, Miss Sherwood," Waddington said grimly. "I didn't want to say anything that might increase my uncle's worries, but the ball is now just two days away."

"I am aware, lieutenant," she said. "Have faith. The

pieces are falling into place."

He nodded with a skepticism to match his uncle's and closed the door.

By the time we reached the waiting carriage, Miss Sherwood had taken on that air of abstraction that I recognized as a sign she was already deep in contemplation of her observations. But I had one last point I wanted to address with her.

"Miss Sherwood," I said as Mary entered the carriage, giving us a moment of relative privacy. "Might I pose one more question before you go?"

"Of course," she said and leveled her clear-eyed gaze at me. "What troubles you?"

"I wouldn't say I was troubled," I said. "I was only wondering if you—" Now that I was saying it out loud, the assertion felt ridiculous. "Did you happen to engage a housekeeper? For me?"

But Miss Sherwood seemed entirely unruffled. "Oh, of course. Mrs. Howell. She comes highly recommended and has worked at the embassy before. I meant to tell you, but with everything that has happened, I forgot. I trust that she is up to your standards."

"Well, yes," I said, feeling as if sand was slipping out from beneath my feet. "She is most competent. I only wondered... that is to say... why?"

"Why?"

"Why did you hire her? Why send her to me?"

"I thought it would give you some peace of mind," she said, simple and to the point. As if the gesture were commonplace and not a singular act of kindness. I blinked at her, nonplussed, and in the course of my gawking noticed a change in her appearance.

"You are not wearing your usual necklace," I said.

Miss Sherwood seemed taken aback by the abrupt

change of topic—quite reasonably so—and her hand drifted to her throat. Where I had become accustomed to seeing her customary snake pendant, she was instead wearing a delicate gold lavalier, which I was able to identify thanks to your fondness for the similar piece that belonged to Mother.

"It was a gift from our grandmother," Miss Sherwood said. "For our sixteenth birthday. Constancia has one, too, and when I saw that she was wearing hers today, I thought I would do likewise." She gave a wistful smile. "It reminded me of when we were young and insisted on dressing alike, despite the fact that no one could tell us apart. Or because of it."

"Ah," I said. "Of course." Though why such a thing would seem obvious enough for me to merit that commentary, I do not know. After an uncomfortable moment, she took pity on me by extending a hand so that I could help her into the conveyance and be left to remonstrate myself in peace.

It returned to work and spent the afternoon occupied with paperwork and a visit to an embassy wife complaining of digestive troubles. It was not until I retired for the evening that I realized I had been half-expecting a message from Miss Sherwood that we would not need to meet in the morning after all, as she had already located the jewels and set everything to rights. I recognized that this sort of expectation was based entirely on my own fancy rather than anything Miss Sherwood had insinuated, but I found that I was still disappointed, and more than a little concerned. Because Waddington had been right. Time is growing short. I hope tomorrow sees things brought to a quick resolution.

Your brother,
Wilf

Chapter 4

23 May 1881

DEAR ESTHER—

After breakfast, I made my way to the office to rendezvous once more with Waddington, then the two of us left for the Sherwood residence. When we were shown into the sitting room, Miss Sherwood was already there waiting as, to my surprise, was Miss Constancia. The ladies rose, greetings were exchanged, and then we all settled around the tea table.

"Well," said Waddington, more brusquely than was really proper. "Have you figured it out?"

"Yes," Miss Sherwood said. "I believe I have."

"And?!" he demanded.

Miss Sherwood narrowed her eyes slightly. Up until this point, they had been cordial to each other in the execution of the investigation—more than cordial even, with Waddington's approval of her request for Lord Marden's funds—but now, cracks were beginning to show. Miss Constancia was not helping matters.

"Well, that's gratitude for you," she said. "My sister is taking it upon herself to sort out the mess your family has made, and you are treating her like a common drudge."

Waddington stared at her coldly, but he did not seem particularly surprised by her brashness. I remembered her description of him on the day of our first meeting— "the disagreeable one who is too handsome for his own good" —and wondered if they had sparred before. Another story for another time, I reasoned. In any case, when Waddington turned his attention back to Miss Sherwood, his jaw was tight, but his tone was more deferent.

"Would you be so good as to explain your findings, Miss Sherwood?"

Miss Sherwood took a moment to smooth her skirts and began, "When we arrived at Lord Marsden's, I made a point of examining the property because I wanted to see if there were any clues around the perimeter of the grounds."

This beginning suggested to me that while she was conceding to Waddington's request, she was going to make him work for it, saving the dramatic revelations for the end; I suspect he recognized this too, but he did not press her further.

"It had rained earlier in the week, and I suspected the damp soil may have had some secrets to divulge. The track leading to the back of the house proved disappointing, but, nearer the kitchen, I could make out impressions that told me a woman had stood there together with a man who left the distinct rounded mark created by a wooden leg in the soil. I could even see that the woman had been startled by something and run off, leaving deep toe and light heel marks, while the man had departed at a more leisurely pace. This scenario was, of course, precisely what had been described to us by Lord Marsden and his niece with regard to Lucy and her beau.

"There was nothing else of note in the area behind the kitchen, but further on, I did make a significant discovery. There was a large patch of flattened vegetation with some blood splattered around on the grass and leaf litter, as well as two sets of footprints, each moving both towards and away from the house. One had been made by a man wearing boots and the other by a different man in bare feet.

"Marsden was barefoot when he was discovered by his father," I said.

Miss Sherwood nodded. "When I inspected the house, I made a point of examining the sill and framework of the hall window just above this spot with my lens. I could at once see that someone had passed out, and could also distinguish the outline of an instep where the barefooted man had come in."

"Could we not simply identify the barefoot man as Marsden at this point?" asked Waddington.

"I think not," said Miss Sherwood. "It would not be precise thinking. I feel confident in my deductions, but I still lack concrete proof."

Miss Constancia sniffed. "Now, shall she continue, or would you like to continue debating semantics?"

"Please go on, Miss Sherwood," I said quickly, hoping to nip this digression in the bud.

"In addition to the information I was able to glean about the barefoot man—" She looked pointedly at Waddington. "I could also tell that the booted man had apparently spent some time in that space outside the window, for the ground had been tamped down by his pacing. I concluded that he had approached the house, waited to interact with someone, then left, and the barefoot man had chased him; while the tread of the booted man indicated that he had walked swiftly in each direction, the barefoot man had run. The flattened vegetation indicated a struggle, obviously. The barefoot man returned to the house afterwards, while the booted man ran off; I saw a few marks continuing on from the house, but I lost his trail after he reached the wall."

"So you think this booted man was responsible for the theft? And that someone inside the house helped him?" said Waddington.

"I do."

"But who in the household would have done such a thing?" I asked.

"Lord and Lady Marsden could safely be eliminated from suspicion, which left only the maids and Miss Holder. And if it were one of the maids, why should Edward allow himself to be accused in their place? There would be no benefit to doing so. But in the case of his cousin…"

"He loves her," I finished. "Lord Marsden told us so."

Waddington groaned and dropped his head to his hands. For her part, Miss Sherwood merely nodded again.

"It is a compelling reason for him to keep her secret—particularly since the secret is such a terrible one. When Lord Marsden revealed he had seen her standing at that very window, the scene became clear. Once she thought her uncle had gone to bed, Miss Holder returned to the window and spoke to the booted man, who was standing out in the lane."

"And what were they discussing?" said Miss Constancia, with a suggestion of interest that was not entirely wholesome.

"Initially? I do not know. They were probably exchanging the usual sweet nothings of clandestine lovers.

But she had something new to share with him—the news that the circlet was on the premises. It was too good an opportunity to pass up. It would have seemed an easy thing for her to slip into the office and get the coronet from the safe."

"But Lord Marsden said that no one knew the combination," I pointed out.

"Edward did. He admitted that he used to break into the safe as a child, simply for the thrill of it; just because Lord Marsden didn't believe him doesn't mean he wasn't telling the truth. And if he knew, and he was devoted to Miss Holder, it makes sense that she would know it, too."

"But how does Edward come into it? Did he know what she was about?"

Miss Sherwood shook her head. "I don't think so. The evidence indicates that following the argument with his father, Edward retreated to his bedroom, fully intending to let the subject rest for the night. But based on what transpired, I suspect that for whatever reason—his anger at his father, his anxiety about his debts—he could not find sleep. So, in the early morning hours, when someone made their way past his room, he heard their footsteps. Curious, he rose and looked out into the hallway, where he saw a stealthy figure make their way down the stairs. Alarmed by the prospect of an intruder, he pulled on his dressing down and went downstairs to investigate. I can only imagine his surprise and dismay when he discovered that the figure was not a burglar at all, but his beloved cousin coming out of Lord Marsden's office with the circlet in her hand.

"Why did he not confront her?"

"I cannot say. I only know that he followed her, presumably skulking in the shadows so as not to be observed, and saw her go to the window. Pushing the curtains aside, she raised the sash, handed the circlet to her lover, then returned everything to its usual state and went back to her room.

"Whatever had prevented him from intervening during the theft, it did not hold enough sway for him to let the circlet vanish into the night. Realizing he needed to act quickly, he ran to the window, threw it open, and leapt out."

"You could see his footprints as well?"

She nodded. "Yes, the impressions of his bare feet are still quite distinct. They indicate that he ran down the lane in pursuit of Sir George Burwell."

My eyebrows shot up. "Sir George?"

Miss Sherwood sipped her tea, giving an affirmative incline of the head. "By every account, Miss Holder went out very little. She seems to have been a very sheltered young lady. One of the few people she saw with some regularity who was not family was Sir George. So the question became, was he the type to woo a naïve young woman who also stood to inherit a substantial amount of money? I knew for a fact that he was."

"You did?" I said. "How?"

She pursed her lips. "You might be surprised what ladies in society talk about when gentlemen are not around to overhear. Miss Holder was not his first conquest. He has made quite a reputation for himself." At this, Miss Constancia let out a snort that served as both agreement and an eloquent, if not strictly ladylike, expression of disgust.

"But Lord Marsden claimed he was a positive influence on Edward," I reminded her, and she pursed her lips looking grim.

"He had been grievously misled on that point. I suspect that neither he nor Edward truly knew the character of the man they had admitted into their family circle. He is a ruined gambler and a blackguard." I glanced at Wadding-ton, but he did not look surprised, nor did he leap to Sir George's defense. Perhaps his uncle and cousin had been ignorant, but he had known.

"Back to the night in question," Miss Sherwood said. "Sir George tried to escape, but he is the shorter and slighter of the two men. Edward caught him, and a struggle ensued. The blood on the ground indicates that at least one of them was hurt in the scuffle, but no one reported any injury on Edward, so I must conclude he inflicted the wound on Sir George. More importantly, each of them fought to get hold of the circlet, and in the resulting tug-of-war, the metal snapped.

"In the heat of the moment, I suspect that Edward did not have a clear idea of what had actually happened. It was a cloudy night, with little visible moonlight, and his temper was running high. But in the ensuing moments, he did understand two things: he still held the circlet, and Sir George had run off into the darkness. He hurried back to the library, hoping to replace the circlet before anyone was the wiser, but when he reached the library, he saw the damage that it had sustained. He immediately set about trying to straighten it, and that is when Lord Marsden discovered him."

Waddington let out a long breath, looking resigned. "Have you located Sir George? Or, more importantly, the jewels?"

"No," said Miss Sherwood. "But I expect that one or both shall be accounted for presently—perhaps by the end of the day." She seemed sanguine enough, but I noticed her response lacked its usual precision. I glanced at her, but her face was impassive.

Waddington got to his feet. "I can't in good conscience make my uncle wait that long for more news.

I shall tell him that a resolution is near at hand but leave off the details related to Clara until we may report definitively that jewels have been recovered to ease the blow." He paused, looking intently as Miss Sherwood. "I don't suppose I need to remind you that time is of the essence."

"You do not," she said evenly, meeting his gaze. After another beat, he nodded, gave the ladies a quick bow, and left.

Once he was gone, I found myself mulling over one point that had not been addressed in Miss Sherwood's explanation. Finally, I could bear it no longer and had to ask.

"There is one thing I still do not understand."

"Oh yes, doctor?" said Miss Sherwood. "What is that?"

"How did Sir George get onto the island without a token?" You may recall, sister, my former description of how unpleasant or even impossible it is to access the island without being granted one of these rare items by the caste. "Presumably Miss Holder has one, but she was in the house the entire time. How was her paramour able to get around without her?"

Miss Sherwood's face took on an expression I couldn't quite read, and she turned to her sister.

"Constancia," she said. "Would you care to illuminate the doctor? After all, I believe you are the one who gave Miss Holder the idea."

For a moment, Miss Constancia did not move. But then she pushed back her shoulders, her expression a combination of contrition and indignation.

"You act as I though I put her up to it on purpose, when all I did was share a humorous anecdote. One that you promised never to bring up again, as I recall."

"And I would happily have kept that promise, if it had

not become relevant to a matter of significant diplomatic importance."

I glanced back and forth between the sisters, utterly at sea.

"I'm sorry, but what are you talking about?"

Miss Constancia sighed. Her hand strayed absently to her pocket, presumably for her cigarettes, but then she moved it back to her lap. Perhaps her sister's chiding had done some good after all.

"A few years back," she began, "there was a big celebration on the island—was it another birthday celebration? Or Yule?" She shifted her gaze up and to the left, considering, then shook her head. "I can't recall. Anyway, you know that in situations such as this, when there are many people from outside the tor coming and going, they issue temporary tokens that are only good for the duration of the event." I had not known that, but I glanced at Miss Sherwood, and she nodded in confirmation. "Well, there was a boy I had met on a visit to my grandparent's estate—the son of the village curate. I liked him quite a lot."

"You mooned over him for months," Miss Sherwood muttered. Miss Constancia shot her a pointed look but continued.

"It had been some time since we had returned from our visit, and I longed to see this boy —let's call him Giacomo."

I raised an eyebrow. "After Casanova?"

"Well, obviously," she said and crossed her ankles demurely. "So, I was missing Giacomo dreadfully, and it occurred to me that with all the commotion that accompanies special occasions on the island, it would be fairly easy for him to slip in unnoticed."

"Provided he had a token," I said, and she nodded.

"So I did what any smitten, enterprising young lady

would do—I bribed the castle official in charge of issuing tokens to add Giacomo to the approved list."

I let out a startled laugh. "And that worked?"

"After a fashion," Miss Constancia said, in a manner that indicated her assertion was a half-truth at best.

"He made it onto the island, and then Father caught them kissing out by the back stretch of the curtain wall," Miss Sherwood said, sounding positively smug.

I coughed and felt my eyes bug, and then it was Miss Constancia's turn to laugh. "Heavens, Dr. Jarvis. Are you alright? I do believe you're blushing."

"I am fine," I said, sounding, admittedly, a bit hoarse. "What happened then?"

Miss Constancia smiled softly, as if the recollection was a pleasant one. "We were both so young. We were also extremely fortunate that it was my father who found us, as he takes a rather more liberal view of these things than many. He dragged us into the house and lectured us about our reckless behavior, then wrote to my grandmother, who sent word back that his family had been frantic when they realized he was missing. Without letting anyone else know, Father took him into Glastonbury and put him on a train home. And that was the last I heard of Giacomo." She sighed wistfully.

"As much as I am enjoying this," Miss Sherwood said, and it truly looked as if she was, "I brought it up for a reason. How did Miss Holder discover your scheme?"

"After she arrived on the island with her uncle, I began noticing her at social gatherings. She looked utterly miserable, but unlike some accommodating guardians with unsociable dependents"— she looked pointedly at Miss Sherwood, who remained tranquil—"he wouldn't let her stay home all the time. I felt sorry for her, so I would strike up conversations with her. Try and get her to smile. One night, I told her the story about Giacomo, though I left out the part about the kissing. She laughed, but she also seemed thoughtful, as if she was turning the story over in her mind. I didn't see her as much after that—I suppose she had made a stronger case to her uncle for abstaining from social obligations. I had honestly forgotten about it, until I heard Honoria discussing the particulars of the circlet situation; then I began to think she had taken my words to heart more than I had realized."

I turned to Miss Sherwood. "So you believe she procured a temporary token, and that is how Sir George was able to get onto the island?"

"I do," she said.

"But how? You don't think *she* bribed an official at the castle, surely."

"She didn't need to. You heard Lord Marsden—she often worked as his secretary. It would have been a simple thing to submit a request in his name without his knowledge."

"Do you mean to say the two of them had planned the theft that far in advance?"

"No," Miss Sherwood replied. "They couldn't have. They didn't know that the circlet would be on the premises. What they were planning to do was run off together, and what a boon the circlet's appearance must have seemed to Sir George. The proceeds from its sale would have been something for them to fall back on while they waited for Lord Marsden to come around to the situation and invite Miss Holder back into the fold, or, in the worst case, to keep them in comfort if the gambit failed and he never came around."

"But Miss Holder is still here," I said. "If they were planning to elope, why wouldn't she have gone with Sir George?"

"It would have been too obvious if they'd disappeared at the same time," said Miss Constancia knowingly.

Miss Sherwood nodded. "My guess is that he went on ahead with the understanding that she would join him at a later time. Whether the disastrous series of events changes that remains to be seen."

"If I were Miss Holder, I would say good riddance," Miss Constancia mused. "A man who cannot even manage a proper elopement is not a man to bind oneself to for life." The clock on the mantle struck the hour, and Miss Constancia winced. "Oh, but I have lost track of time. The dressmaker will be here shortly for my final fitting; I should go. Good afternoon, doctor."

I rose with her and bowed as she departed, then reclaimed my seat and picked up the previous line of conversation.

"If there is still a chance that Miss Holder could bolt, that makes it even more urgent to reclaim the gems and return them to Lord Marsden. So where are they now?"

"I do not know," said Miss Sherwood, and her eyes dropped to her skirts, which she again made a point of smoothing.

I stared at her. "You don't?"

"No. It is the one aspect of the case that remains opaque to me."

I ran a hand over my hair. "But after everything you've learned, you must have some idea?"

"Well, of course I have some idea," she said sharply, and her gaze flicked back up to me. "But 'some idea' is not the same as knowing. And I am missing some key pieces of information that would allow me to determine the location with certainty."

My mind was awhirl, attempting to take in the implications of this admission. "You assured Waddington that the gems' return was imminent. And you have the cheque from Lord Marsden… all that money…."

Miss Sherwood's eyes flashed. "Have you so little faith in me, doctor? That I would commit to a particular outcome without confidence that I would be able to see it through to its conclusion?"

"No," I protested. "I have complete faith in your abilities. There just seem to be so many loose ends—"

Abruptly, Miss Sherwood got to her feet. "This audience has run rather longer than I expected," she said, voice steely. "And I have much to do to tie up these 'loose ends'. I think it would be best if you left, so that I may accomplish that at speed."

I sat gaping at her for a moment, but eventually, I snapped my hanging jaw shut and rose to my feet.

"I apologize for whatever I have done to offend you," I said quietly, and then I turned and left the room. Miss Sherwood did not say anything further, and she did not follow.

I confess that I was flummoxed and not a little affronted by this turn of events. This bout of temper is most unlike her; the only time I have seen anything comparable is the time Waddington called her a meddling female and I—admittedly—was not the ally to her I should have been. But if there was an insult here, I am ignorant of it. I do believe that she will salvage this disaster of a situation, and if I expressed reservations, it is only because my intellect is not as cunningly sharp as her own. In truth, I can think of no one who is her equal, which makes her outrage all the more frustrating. This cannot be a new experience for her. She must have contended with it for most of her life. So why did I merit such hostility?

Returning to work, I holed up in my office, where I could brood in peace, interrupted only once or twice when

Pryce needed help to field a ball-related emergency. He still has not mentioned the circlet, which presumably means the secretary-ambassador's office has somehow kept the situation under wraps, but that pretense cannot hold for much longer; the ball is tomorrow, and I have not received any message indicating that Miss Sherwood found the jewels as promised. Cold logic tells me I should be bracing for the discovery of the theft in a professional capacity, but I find that my personal grievances are consuming just as much of my attention, if not more. For now, there is little I can do on either front, so I plan to indulge once more in Collins, but this time more to find more solace than enjoyment.

Your petulant brother,
Wilf

Chapter 5

24 May 1881

DEAR ESTHER—

I awoke in a foul temper. There had still been no word from Miss Sherwood, and the day promised to be long, arduous, and messy. I stewed as I went about my morning routine, dragging my feet as I went, and it did nothing for my mood when I went to break my fast and found Mrs. Howell in the kitchen.

She had been arranging food on a tray, but when she saw me, she began transferring it over to the dining table. I had to admit that the meal smelled delicious, so I gingerly made my way over and had a seat. As she finished, I noticed that she had pulled a stool I had never seen before up to the counter. In a flash, I realized the difficulty she must have had in utilizing a kitchen - an entire house, in fact - that did not feature any of the accommodations I had noticed elsewhere on the island that allowed brownies to effectively navigate spaces built for those of greater stature. I did not necessarily feel a personal sense of responsibility on this score—after all, I had only lived in the cottage for a few months, and I had not anticipated Mrs. Howell's presence in it—but I was aware of a sort of second-hand shame on behalf of the embassy community. Brownies carry out much of the domestic work on the island, for human and Folk alike; failing to account for that reality in buildings constructed in the Quarter seemed heedless at best, callous at worst. I felt my mood soften a little as she set my plate in front of me.

"Thank you, Mrs. Howell," I said and felt a fresh stab of conscience when she seemed surprised at the acknowledgement.

"Well, get on with you," she said, covering her reaction. "You're far too thin. No one will take you seriously as a figure of authority if you look like you'd blow away in a stuff wind."

I accepted the admonishment without comment and obeyed the command. The food tasted just as good as it smelled, and by the time I finished, I was feeling slightly better.

"That was delicious, Mrs. Howell," I said when I finally pushed my chair back. "Thank you again. Truly."

She nodded as she cleared my plate, but once she had moved it to the sink, she turned back, considering me.

"I must confess, doctor," she said at length. "That I wasn't quite sure about this posting at first. You did not seem as if you would be a particularly courteous or considerate employer."

Feeling duly chastened, I said, "And yet you stayed on. Why?"

She nodded thoughtfully. "It was that Miss Sherwood engaged me. She has always struck me as a lady of discernment and good character. I trusted that she would not have sent me if the position were a bad one."

"Do you know Miss Sherwood well?" I said.

"Oh, no," she said, as if the very idea was ludicrous. "She is a wight, on her mother's side at least, and their kind rarely mingle with ours. But you know—servants talk." This was said with such utter frankness, despite the obvious implication of who they talk about, that I had to smile.

"And do you plan to stay in the position now? Does it meet with your approval?"

She looked at me over the tops of her spectacles and sniffed. "It will do."

With that settled, I made my way over to the office, braced for whatever might transpire. I was gloomily making my way through a stack of paperwork when there was a rap on my open office door. I'm not exactly sure who I was expecting it to be, but it was definitely not the figure who stood there when I lifted my gaze—Robin Goodfellow.

"May I come in?" he said.

"Oh, yes, of course." I leapt to my feet, gesturing to the chair opposite me. "Please have a seat."

He did, and once settled, we sat in somewhat uncomfortable silence, until he finally said, "I suppose you're wondering why I'm here."

"I am, sir," I admitted.

"It is only that Honoria came to see me yesterday."

"Oh?"

"She needed my assistance with a plan of hers to reclaim the jewels that had gone missing. Seeing as we only very nearly avoided a catastrophe of international proportions a few months ago, I did what I could."

"And did that plan succeed? Was she able to procure her quarry?"

He waved a hand. "I believe those particulars are hers to share. My aim today has more to do with the conduct she described in relation to yourself when you expressed reservations about her efforts."

I raised my eyebrows in surprise and not a little indignation. What business was our encounter of his? "How so?"

He paused, considering his words. "I think you know by now that Honoria is rather exceptional. You've seen the way she can read a situation in a way that no one else can, uncover connections no one else can see. And thanks to the legacy of two almost painfully capable and assertive parents, she has a will of iron. Sometimes, when she is aroused by some strong emotion, these qualities lead her to take actions that may strike others as excessive."

"If she is in fact this creature you describe," I said. "It seems to me that she should be capable of fighting her own battles rather than relying on a proxy."

Goodfellow inclined his head, conceding the point. "She is. And I doubt she would thank me, if she knew I had come. But you must understand, doctor—she is the closest thing I have had to a daughter. It is difficult for me not to step in if I see she is in pain."

That gave me pause. "Pain?"

He nodded, brow furrowed. He was quiet for a moment, as if considering his words, before he replied.

"I have known Honoria for quite a long time. I have come to understand something of how her mind works, though heaven knows there are depths I would never deign to reach. While she did not say so out loud, I believe that she is terribly afraid of disappointing you."

I stared at him in astonishment. "*Disappoint* me?" As if such a thing was possible.

He nodded again. "For most of her life, Honoria's intellect has been treated as something of a novelty, and that is when it was not seen as bizarre or outright danger- ous; even her parents, for all that they love her, often don't know what to make of her. Excepting Constancia, you are unique in actually admiring that intellect and her for putting it to constructive use When she was unable to meet every challenge related to the circlet situation with her preferred speed and efficiency, I think she worried that she would be diminished in your eyes."

"But that is nonsense!" I protested. "What she accom- plished was nothing short of extraordinary, and even if she had not been able to piece together the story for Lord Marsden, I could never have thought any less of her."

"I believe you," he said. "And I believe Honoria would, too, in time. But even a soul as rational and methodical as hers is not immune to the specters of fear and loneliness."

My initial impulse was to snap back at Goodfellow, insist that he was mistaken. After a moment's considera- tion, though, I found that his theory held water. Thinking back over the last few days, I remembered instances of Miss Sherwood reacting in ways that seemed out of char- acter, hanging back a bit, when normally she would stride forward. As I had in my kitchen that morning, I cursed myself for a villain.

I sighed. "So what do you propose I do?"

"You are a grown man possessed of free will—it is not my place to dictate," he said, getting to his feet. "But I will pass along the information that Honoria is scheduled to call at the Marsden residence at ten o'clock to meet with the secretary ambassador." His mien remained serious, but there was a twinkle in his eye which carried a suggestion of the impish Puck about it. "Good day, Dr. Jarvis."

After he left, I sat at my desk for a long time considering his words. Then I took out my pocket watch to check the time. It was half-past nine—leaving just enough time for me to reach Lord Marsden's house in time for the meeting. With a sigh, I replaced my watch and got to my feet. As I left the office, I called to Pryce that I was going out, and then I headed to the meeting.

I arrived with some time to spare and decided to linger on the high street rather than approach the house, lest I be mistaken for one of Lucy's admirers. As such, when a carriage appeared at precisely ten o'clock, I was close enough to open the door for the occupants before the driver was able to hop down from the box. When Miss Sherwood caught sight of me, her eyes widened, but then her face went carefully blank, giving me no indication of how my presence had been received as I helped her down.

"What are you doing here?" she said as Mary disembarked behind her.

"I thought having an ally with you might give you some peace of mind," I said. Still, her face was unreadable, but she nodded, and as we made our way up to the door, she fell into step beside me.

At our knock, the door swung open to reveal Waddington, looking as grim as I'd yet seen him.

"Come in," he said with a sigh. "There's been a new development."

He escorted us to the now familiar drawing room, then excused himself to retrieve his uncle. When the two of them appeared a few minutes later, I was alarmed by the change that had come over the secretary ambassador. He'd been displaying signs of strain, but now he barely seemed able to keep to his feet. He greeted us shakily and dropped into a nearby chair, passing a hand over his face. I glanced first at Waddington and then at Miss Sherwood, trying to determine their thoughts.

"Are you well, my lord?" Miss Sherwood said finally.

Lord Marsden gave a humorless laugh and looked up into our inquiring faces. "I do not know what I have done," he said, "to be so severely tried. Only a few days ago, all was well in my world. Now, my professional life is in shambles, my family in tatters. First Edward departed, and now Clara has deserted me."

"Deserted you?" I repeated, glancing at Miss Sherwood.

Lord Marsden nodded and produced a slip of paper from his pocket.

"When Lucy went to build a fire in her room this morning, the bed had not been slept in, the wardrobe was empty, and a note for me lay upon the hall table. I had said to Clara last night—in sorrow, mind you, not in anger—that if she had only agreed to marry Edward, all of this might have been avoided. Perhaps it was thoughtless of me to say so. It is that remark which she refers to in this note."

Waddington, who had presumably already read the note, passed it to Miss Sherwood, who held it between us so that we might read it at the same time.

MY DEAREST UNCLE,—I *feel that I have brought trouble upon you, and that if I had acted differently this terrible misfortune might never have occurred. I cannot, with this thought in my mind, ever again be happy under your roof, and I feel that I must leave you forever. Do not worry about my future, for that is provided for; and, above all, do not search for me, for it will be fruitless labor and an ill-service to me. In life or in death, I am ever your loving CLARA*

. . .

MISS SHERWOOD GLANCED at me to confirm that I had read all, and when I nodded, she folded the missive and passed it back to Lord Marsden.

"What could she mean by that note, Miss Sherwood?" he asked, voice trembling. "You do not think that it points to…to suicide?"

"Oh, no," she rushed to assure him. "Nothing like that. However the truth may grieve you, you may rest assured that she has not taken her own life."

This seemed to mollify him, but only a little. "What truth? Speak plainly, I beg you."

"Very well," she said, her voice gentle. "It was Clara who was responsible for the disappearance of the jewels, along with Sir George Burnwell. There has been an understanding between them for, I believe, a good while. They have now fled together."

If possible, Lord Marsden went even paler. "That cannot be!"

"I assure you it can," Miss Sherwood said in that same placating tone. "By all accounts, Sir George is a charming and charismatic man, and your niece is a rather sheltered young lady who, as your adopted daughter and one so dear to your heart, also stands to inherit a goodly sum upon your death."

"But Sir George is the most honorable of men," Lord Marsden protested. "He would never perpetrate such a ruse." At this, Waddington rose and went to the window.

"I am afraid you have been misled regarding the caliber of Sir George's character," said Miss Sherwood. "Clara is not the first young woman he has seduced; he is well-practiced at the art of persuasion. When he professed his love to her, she became irrevocably bound to him. And so when she told him of the circlet in your possession, and he bade her steal it, she could not resist."

"But it was Edward I saw holding the circlet," Lord Marsden protested weekly. "Not Clara."

"I will lay it out for you," Miss Sherwood said, and she went on to detail for Lord Marsden everything she had explained in her sitting room the day before. Lord Marsden listened attentively, but at the conclusion of her tale, he fell back in his chair, looking exhausted.

"And that is why Clara fainted when she saw the circlet in Edward's hands," he said, more to himself than to us. "Because she knew their plan had been foiled, at least partially. But if Edward knew, why did he not say anything? Why not reveal the true culprits?"

"Because," Miss Sherwood said, "by your own admission, he loved one of the culprits. He could not tell the truth without, in his mind, betraying Clara."

"But that is nonsense!" Lord Marsden sputtered. "He did not owe her that silence!"

"I agree," said Miss Sherwood. "Edward took a more charitable view, however, and kept her secret."

Lord Marsden dropped his head to his hands. "Oh, but I am a fool. A fool! I raged at him, treated him like a common criminal, and he was doing his best to protect all of us. He is a better son than I deserve."

"Yes," Miss Sherwood said, but only an observation, not a judgment. "Like all of us, he may have his foibles, but he is endeavoring to be a good man—the man you urged him to be. And it was not the influence of a compatriot that accomplished that effort. It was his own will and tenacity that did it."

Lord Marsden sat quiet for a moment, then rose and strode to the sideboard, which boasted an impressive collection of liquor bottles. Paying no heed to the early hour, he poured a slug of whiskey into a handy tumbler and took it down in one gulp. Setting the glass down, he peered into the middle distance for a moment before turning back to the company at large.

"I am most grateful for all of your efforts, Miss Sherwood. And there is some comfort in knowing the truth of what transpired. But there has been little material change to my position. The jewels are still missing. The embassy—and, by extension, the Empire—will be subjected to scorn and derision, and I will have to face the bitter reality that I am largely to blame."

"Well, on that point at least," Miss Sherwood said, opening her reticule and withdrawing a small parcel. "All may not be as dire as you imagine."

She held out the parcel to him, and with a furrowed brow, he strode forward to take it. After making quick work of the paper wrapping, he opened the box and gasped.

"You found them," he said and lifted the broken piece of the circlet into the light, the jewels winking in their settings.

"I did," she said. "And I believe there is time for a Folk smith to patch the damage before the ball so that no one is the wiser."

After bearing such a weight for days, the lightening of it was seemingly too much for Lord Marsden. A tear ran down his cheek into his mustache.

"Thank you, Miss Sherwood. Thank you. I am forever in your debt."

She gave a smile that was kind yet incisive. "If there is a debt to be repaid, it is to your son. You still have a chance to set things right with him, and I would only consider your obligations unmet if you neglected to take it. Now, let us make a plan for the circlet's repair."

As they spoke, I noticed that Waddington had slipped out the door leading to the garden. Curious, I went after him and found him standing on the terrace, smoking a cigarette. At my approach, he glanced up and grunted an acknowledgment.

"This must have been a very difficult few days for you," I said, and he gave a mirthless laugh.

"You could say that."

"I must say that you have acquitted yourself very well. You must have been a great comfort and support to your uncle."

He gave another bitter chuckle and dropped the end of the cigarette, extinguishing it with the toe of his boot before turning away from me to stare out over the grounds.

"Do you know what the worst of it was?"

"No," I replied.

"It was seeing how easily he accused Edward, and how easily he was able to believe the best of Sir George." He paused, shoving his hands in his pockets. "It has always been like that. We were never good enough, Edward and me. My uncle, my father, everyone of their generation would hold Sir George, or someone like him, up as a paragon of who we should be. They told Clara that he was the kind of man she should aspire to wed. And for what? When the chips were down, and Sir George proved to be a bounder and a blackguard, it was Edward who took action to protect our uncle and, by extension, the family. It was me my uncle turned to in his hour of greatest need. The paragon, meanwhile, has damaged my cousin's reputation so thoroughly that she may never recover. And it means nothing. My uncle still sees us as misbehaving boys, not men. The circlet will be restored, and everything will go on as it has before."

"Maybe not," I said. "He seemed to heed Miss Sherwood's urging to seek out Edward and make things right."

"Perhaps," he said and was still a while before turning

without another word and returning to the house. After a moment, I followed. We did not speak of the matter again that day.

Once Miss Sherwood and Lord Marsden were satisfied with a plan of action regarding the circlet, Miss Sherwood placed it in her reticule, and the women made ready to leave. Lord Marsden, looking more peaceful than he had since the whole ordeal had begun but also as if he could easily fall into bed and sleep for hours, bade us farewell. I believed our meeting had reached its conclusion, but as we made our way down the front walk to the carriage, Miss Sherwood paused.

"You know, the weather is so fine today," she said. "I find that I should like to walk. If it is all right with Mary, that is."

"Of course, miss," Mary said. She spoke evenly, but I thought I caught something in her expression that looked like approval. I seemed to have passed some kind of test.

The carriage departed, and we began to make our way to the high street. Miss Sherwood and I strolled side by side, while Mary followed at the maximum distance that would still be considered sufficient for a chaperon. I felt confident that any conversation between Miss Sherwood and myself would not be overheard, and I was grateful for it. But then I had a hard time coming up with anything to say.

"Lord Marsden seems to have had more than enough excitement for the foreseeable future," I came up with finally, cringing at how awkward and forced my words sounded to my own ears.

"I daresay you are correct," Miss Sherwood replied. We walked on in silence for another minute or two before I found I could not contain my curiosity any longer.

"How did you locate the jewels? I have been wondering ever since you showed them to Lord Marsden."

"It seemed obvious that Sir George would try to sell the jewels," she said. "My reluctance to elaborate on that theory yesterday was owing to the overwhelming number of options he had for doing so. I had nothing concrete to suggest where he might go to undertake the sale, or when, or why. In the end, the only option was to start looking for the jewels nearby and then venture further afield if necessary."

"So, what did you do?"

"Constancia, Mary, and I donned male attire and went into Glastonbury, visiting merchants and pawnbrokers in the guise of men to see if any of them had acquired the jewels."

Over the course of my acquaintance with Miss Sherwood, I believed I had become accustomed to her startling pronouncements and able to accept them with some degree of equanimity. Even so, all I could do was goggle at her in astonishment.

"You did what?!"

"I was going to invite you to accompany us," she said, apparently as some sort of defense, "but, well…"

I took a deep breath to collect myself. We both knew why she hadn't asked me.

"It worked, though. You were able to find the stones."

She nodded. "It was not a straightforward endeavor, I assure you. We began with some of the more upscale, respectable establishments and found very little."

"It does seem that those would be the first places Sir George would visit," I said. "They would presumably give him the greatest return on his investment."

"Oh, he tried," she said. "The last merchant we visited

finally admitted as much. But they are not fools, those businessmen. They knew something was not quite right. The jewels were not loose, after all, but still contained in their broken setting. Even if the shopkeepers did not recognize them as being part of the circlet, they could tell they weren't dealing with legitimate goods. They did not want any of the legal trouble they knew must be hounding him. So they refused to buy."

"So what did he do? And how did you find them?"

"The last merchant, the one who revealed that Sir George had visited him, gave me the name and address of an individual less troubled by scruples in his business dealings, a fellow named Ronan Norris. Rather than operating a reputable storefront on the high street, he worked out of the back room of a pub near the well house on the edge of town. He was also not the type to keep regular hours, which suited us fine, as by the time we found him, it was getting quite late."

I felt color drain from my face but managed to maintain my composure. "And he had them."

She nodded, and the corner of her mouth quirked up in a wry smile. "He did. And it turned out that he had only paid Sir George £600 per stone. But he had us at a disadvantage, and I ended up having to forfeit the full amount Lord Marsden had given me to get the stones back."

"And how did you manage it? Surely you didn't just give him the cheque."

"Oh, no," she said. "I went to Robin and had him advance me the amount in hard currency from the castle accounts. I would have returned it if we had come up empty-handed, but now he will be able to draw the funds from Lord Marsden's account."

Thinking of the women navigating the underbelly of Glastonbury alone with that much cash, made me come over a bit faint, no matter what kind of disguises they were wearing, But I supposed everything had come out all right in the end: they were all back on the island, safe and sound; Lord Marsden had been dealt a blow by the conduct of his niece, but also gained an opportunity to mend fences with his son; and a further crisis in the relations between the Seelie Court and Great Britain had been averted. All that was left was the tension that remained between Miss Sherwood and myself.

As I ruminated, she glanced back to check on Mary, and I caught a glimpse of her throat. Her snake necklace was back. At the sight of it, I recalled the verse she said gave her direction in life.

Be ye therefore wise as serpents and harmless as doves.

I thought of Goodfellow's words to me that morning. A harmless dove was well and good, I realized, but without some sort of protection (aside from a well-meaning sister), it would be devoured by predators, and I felt an almost painful stab of tenderness. Of course she would try to protect herself. And of course she would not want to be defined by only a single aspect of her being.

I was casting about within my mind for something to ease the conversation in a direction related to something besides the sapphire circlet when Miss Sherwood said. "I would like to apologize for my conduct yesterday."

"Oh?" I said, and she nodded.

"It was shabby of me."

"It is all right," I said.

"No, it is not," she said. "But it is kind of you to say so."

We walked on in silence a bit longer, but a comfortable one this time. At length, I decided to ask her something that had perplexed me.

"If Miss Holder has gone off with Sir George, what

will happen to her? £1800 is a goodly amount, but it won't last forever, and they must realize that her inheritance is forfeit at this point. Will Sir George stand by her or throw her over for some other lucrative match?"

"I do not know," she said. "I suspect it will be the latter, but perhaps Sir George will surprise us."

"Based on what you have said of him, I'm not sure which option would be the more favorable outcome for her."

"Nor I," said Miss Sherwood. "But that is often the way of it. A lady's circumstances often come down to the inclinations of a man who seeks to gain something from her. As her uncle said, though, her regret may be compounded by the knowledge that she was a willing participant in her downfall."

I glanced at her. "You think her deserving of that punishment?"

"'Deserving' does not enter into it," she said. "She sought love, as do we all, but she chose poorly. She will suffer for that choice; however, she has also caused suffering. There are scales there to be balanced. How that is achieved remains to be seen."

We had by now reached the retaining wall that marks the transition from the British Quarter to the bustling commercial district, and Miss Sherwood brought us to a halt.

"You needn't venture any further with us," she said. "We can make the remainder of the journey on our own."

"Are you certain?" I said.

Miss Sherwood smiled. "Yes. After navigating the more unsavory areas of Glastonbury at night, this will be a simple thing."

I had really meant to confirm her desire to continue on

unaccompanied rather than question her capability, but I smiled wryly at her remark. By this time, Mary had almost reached us, which meant our conversation was coming to a close.

"Will you be at the ball tonight?" she asked

"Yes," I said. "Nearly all embassy staff will be there. Attendance is expected as a matter of protocol, but even if that weren't the case, everyone is excited about the prospect of seeing Princess Beatrice."

Miss Sherwood nodded. "Then I will be sure to save you a dance."

I felt a distinct sweeping sensation in my stomach at her words. To cover my heightened emotion, I bowed over her hand.

"I look forward to it."

Mary joined us then, and after an exchange of farewells, they mounted the stairs in the curtain wall, while I made my way back into the Quarter.

The remainder of the workday felt painfully long, devoted, as it was, to the completion of the paperwork I had abandoned earlier in the day. But aside from the inevitable tedium of that task, I found myself anxious to be finished because I was looking forward to the social event this evening, a feeling I have never experienced in my time on the island and possibly in my entire life. When I finally left for the day, I felt like a schoolboy released from his lessons. And when I arrived home, I found a plate of freshly baked scones waiting for me on the counter. Truly, Mrs. Howell is a wizard of a baker. Despite the upheaval of the week, I find that I am in better spirits than I have been in a long time.

And now, I must put down my pen and go get dressed. After all, there is a dance card with my name on it.

Your brother,
Wilf

━━

WILF, *Honoria, and the other residents of Ynis Within will return.*

IN THE MEANTIME, *you can sign up for my newsletter to get information about new releases, cool extras, and other fun stuff at www.reneeedwardsauthor.com.*

Author's Note

This book required significantly less research than the first in the Sherwood & Jarvis series, *A Puzzle of Poppies*, and my approach to the research that was called for had a certain lepidopterous* quality - flitting around from flower to flower, never staying one place too long. There were a couple of books related to Constancia's artistic predilections, though, that I'd like to recognize as coming in particularly handy: *Bohemian London: From Thomas De Quincey to Jeffrey Bernard* by Travis Elborough and *Wilde's Women: How Oscar Wilde Was Shaped by the Women He Knew* by Eleanor Fitzsimons.

More tasty historical minutiae next time, perhaps...

Renee Edwards
   2024

———

*Did you know that "lepidopterous" means "of or relating to butterflies"? Now you do.

About the Author

Renee is a lifelong book person and trained librarian. Her favorite books to read are the kind with magic, adventure, and romance, so those are what she set out to write. She fiddles away on her laptop in Texas, where she lives with her husband and a basset hound named Winifred.

Also by Renee Edwards

A POWERFUL PROHIBITION

To the Stars

SHERWOOD & JARVIS

A Puzzle of Poppies